"You don't s
Lizzie said,

"Just Damien," he told her, straightening. "And you lie, Lizzie. I scare you to death."

Lizzie stared up at him, mesmerized by his shadowed face, by the grim, lost beauty of him. There was something about his eyes. They seemed to call to her across decades. She'd looked into those eyes long, long ago, in another lifetime, another world.

She took a deep breath. "Is there any way you could stop the article from running?"

"Not even if I wanted to. But I'll give you a piece of advice. Get out of town. Go someplace where the streets don't run with blood. Go as far away as you can until this madman is caught."

"I can't," she whispered, still staring at him.

"Then may God have mercy on your soul, Elizabeth Stride," he said, his voice sounding centuries old.

Dear Reader,

Welcome once again to the dark side of love. Shadows has only been around for a few memorable months, but I have to say that our lineup this month is one of the strongest I can imagine.

Anne Stuart is a name fans of romance and suspense are highly familiar with, and everyone knows that her name on the cover of a book means you'll get only the best on the pages inside. Now, in *Break the Night,* she's outdone herself. This book has it all: an eerie moodiness, a shiveringly sensuous tone, a darkly compelling story line you'll race to finish and characters who practically step off the pages into real life. Theirs is a romance you won't be able to resist—nor will you want to! I have only three more words to say to you about this book: Don't miss it!

Rachel Lee is one of Silhouette's newest stars, but already she's a veteran of the bestseller list. Now, with her first Shadows title, she demonstrates anew why her reputation has grown so quickly. *Imminent Thunder* is set during the sultry Florida storm season. The air is thick, breathing is difficult, and your heart will pound not only with passion, but from fear for the future, as Honor Nightingale and Ian McLaren search for solutions to the mystery of who is shadowing Honor, haunting her house and sifting through her most intimate thoughts in an attempt to drive her mad—or worse.

The months to come will be just as exciting, with books by authors like Helen R. Myers, Lori Herter, Carla Cassidy, Barbara Faith, Jane Toombs and more. There's always irresistible reading waiting for you in the shadows . . . Silhouette Shadows.

Yours,

Leslie J. Wainger
Senior Editor and Editorial Coordinator

ANNE STUART

BREAK THE NIGHT

Published by Silhouette Books New York
America's Publisher of Contemporary Romance

SILHOUETTE BOOKS
300 East 42nd St., New York, N.Y. 10017

BREAK THE NIGHT

Copyright © 1993 by Anne Kristine Stuart Ohlrogge

All rights reserved. Except for use in any review, the reproduction or utilization of this work in whole or in part in any form by any electronic, mechanical or other means, now known or hereafter invented, including xerography, photocopying and recording, or in any information storage or retrieval system, is forbidden without the permission of the publisher, Silhouette Books, 300 E. 42nd St., New York, N.Y. 10017

ISBN: 0-373-27009-7

First Silhouette Books printing June 1993

All the characters in this book have no existence outside the imagination of the author and have no relation whatsoever to anyone bearing the same name or names. They are not even distantly inspired by any individual known or unknown to the author, and all incidents are pure invention.

® and ™:Trademarks used with authorization. Trademarks indicated with ® are registered in the United States Patent and Trademark Office, the Canada Trade Mark Office and in other countries.

Printed in the U.S.A.

Books by Anne Stuart

Silhouette Shadows

Break the Night #9

Silhouette Intimate Moments

Special Gifts #321
Now You See Him... #429

ANNE STUART

was first published at age seven in *Jack and Jill* magazine. She wrote her first novel in 1974, and has since published in a variety of genres, including Gothic, Regency, suspense and contemporary romance. She particularly likes the spice of danger mixed with the emotional turmoil of romance. She currently lives in the mountains of Vermont with her husband and two children.

PROLOGUE

The sky over Los Angeles was bloodred.

At first they thought it was a new form of toxic waste. Red smog, caused by a combination of industrial exhaust and the peculiar weather conditions. A good stiff wind would blow everything away in just a matter of time.

But the red sky continued, and the scientists began to debate. It had to have been caused by the latest nuclear accident, or perhaps by brushfires burning out of control. Maybe even an act of God.

The historians were no comfort. The red sky had been recorded throughout the past, from France in the fourteen hundreds, when Gilles de Retz cut a bloody path through the countryside, to London in the fall of 1888, when Jack the Ripper made his rounds, to Germany in 1905, when Peter Kurten, the Düsseldorf Ripper, carved his way through a terrified populace.

The Santa Ana winds blew hot and dry from the desert, swirling down from the bloodred sky, and suicide rates tripled. The endless storms followed, drenching the sprawling cityscape. And somewhere in the dark, rain-soaked streets of Venice, California, Springheeled Jack, Saucy Jack, Jack the Ripper, made one of his periodic appearances. And the streets ran red with blood, so much blood that not even the rain could wash it clean.

CHAPTER ONE

Lizzie Stride pushed her hair away from her face, leaving a streak of red paint across her high cheekbone. It was too hot in her studio apartment, but she couldn't afford to turn up the air-conditioning. She couldn't open any windows, either—the rain had been falling nonstop for days now, and even her skin felt moldy. Running the dehumidifier already ate up about half her electricity allowance—she couldn't afford to crank up the air conditioner besides.

As long as her work survived, she could sit there and suffer. No one melted from a little heat and humidity, even if it felt as if she might. What mattered was the mask beneath her hands as she smoothed and shaped the red-tinged clay over the heavy eyebrows. If anything, the weather was good for it, keeping the material pliant for a longer period of time. Long enough for her to decide exactly how she wanted to shape this one. How to perfect it.

She took several deep, calming breaths. Surely she could lower her steamy body temperature by meditating. The mind was infinitely powerful—she just hadn't learned how to harness hers. She could hear Kate Bush on the radio, singing something eerie, a fitting counterpoint to the face beneath her fingertips. It had turned evil beneath her hands, as her masks had done far too often of late. She didn't tend to waste much time analyzing her work. Each face grew on its own beneath her long, deft fingers. Sometimes a clown, all garish colors and absurd features, sometimes a diva with ostrich feathers and jewels. And sometimes a fiend from hell.

. Unfortunately, the monsters sold better than the other, more frivolous masks. It was no wonder, she thought, shoving her hair back yet again. The world was full of human monsters, and L.A. had more than its share.

They'd found the sixth body two days ago in a Dumpster in Venice, and within hours she'd been trapped at the police station once more, trying to make sense of a random savagery that should have had no connection to her at all. Except for the fact that each victim was wearing one of her masks when the body was found.

The Venice Ripper, they were calling him. Fortunately, the newspapers didn't know about the masks, or about the truly horrifying details of the medically accurate butchery of the prostitute-victims. Lizzie was still anonymous enough, an innocent pulled into the horror by her art and by a madman's random appreciation.

When the police had traced the second mask to her, she'd stopped working for a while—too horrified by the piece of evidence she'd identified. The blood-soaked papier-mâché had once been a Kewpie-doll face, and the knowledge that the killer had used her masks during his bizarre killing spree made her feel sick inside, like an unwilling accessory to the madman.

But stopping her work, hiding in her apartment when she wasn't making ends meet as a waitress at the Pink Pelican Café, did no good at all. She'd made a lot of masks in the two years she'd been in the Los Angeles area. And sold a fair number. And the killer seemed to have an inexhaustible supply.

She sat back, staring at the mask beneath her fingers. The red streaks looked like blood, the mouth was open in a silent, hideous scream, and somewhere a killer waited—one of her masks in his murderous hands.

Kate Bush stopped singing. The news came on, a muffled voice, one she didn't want to hear. The Ripper had claimed another victim, the body found dumped behind a building near the beach.

And Lizzie brought her fists down on the mask, crushing it beneath her strong hands.

Damien stood at the window overlooking the gray, endless city, his long fingers wrapped tightly around a mug of coffee. He'd lost weight in the past couple of months, more than was good for him. And it was no wonder—he subsisted on a diet of black coffee, straight tequila, cigarettes and fast food. When he remembered to eat. Most of the time he forgot.

It was all right, though. He'd grown soft in the past few years. Life could do that to you. Too many awards, too much money, and things got a little too easy.

Not that they were easy for him now. He'd left his job at the *Chronicle* after the second Ripper murder. After the second nightmare. Left his Pulitzer and his retirement fund and his beautiful, intelligent research assistant who'd let him know she was interested in doing more than his legwork, left behind the toughest, fairest editor in the business. Left behind a weekly paycheck, and his only connection to sanity.

None of that mattered. None of the safe, comfortable things he'd worked for made any difference to him any longer. He was a man possessed, driven, with only one need in life. To find the Ripper. And stop him.

He looked at his reflection in the rain-streaked glass. Gaunt, unshaven cheeks, dark, tormented eyes, hair long and shaggy. The Ripper probably looked a great deal like him. Haunted. Hunted. Driven.

Damien leaned his forehead against the grimy window, staring out into the bleak twilight before he shut his eyes. Only to see the blood once more, and hear the scream of the dying woman. The sound that would live in his mind forever. And he smashed his forehead against the glass, once, twice, until he heard the window crack.

The apartment was still and silent hours later when Lizzie let herself back in, locking the door behind her. She'd turned off the air-conditioning before she left, and the accumulated heat and dampness swept over her like a wave. She leaned against the door, not bothering to turn on the light. She could smell the clay from the smashed mask, the bitter, oily odor from that morning's coffee, mixed with the memory of yesterday's pasta. She almost wished for the hot, dry desert winds to sweep through, clearing away the constant, heavy rain.

"We'll be glad to give you police protection," Detective Finlay Adamson, the middle-aged, coffee-guzzling, avuncular police lieutenant working on the Ripper case, had told Lizzie when he drove her back to her apartment late that afternoon. This time they'd kept her only three hours, going over the same old unanswerable questions. "I don't think you're in any particular danger—this psycho only goes for prostitutes, and he'd have no reason to hurt you. For what it's worth, the police psychiatrist thinks he considers you some kind of ally, and—"

"Please, don't!" Lizzie had begged him, the nausea rising. "It's not my fault that some monster uses my masks."

"Calm down, Miss Stride. No one's blaming you," Adamson said in his patient voice.

"But can't you see, I'm blaming myself? As far as I know, no one's bought more than two or three masks of mine. I've asked everyone who sells them for me, and no one remembers making any more sales than that. Are you certain you've checked all the galleries and gift shops?"

"You wouldn't believe how many times we've checked," Adamson said wearily. "The kind of place that carries your stuff isn't great on keeping records. We're just lucky we found you in the first place. A reporter happened to recognize one of the murder masks as yours. Apparently he has a couple of them himself."

The sick feeling in Lizzie's stomach didn't subside. "A reporter who collects masks? Who's covering the Ripper murders? Doesn't that strike you as a little too coincidental? Are you sure . . . ?"

"Don't do my job for me, Miss Stride. Everyone's a suspect in this case, even the most unlikely people. Including yourself. We haven't discounted Damien, even if it doesn't seem possible."

"Damien?"

"Used to write for the *Chronicle*. J. R. Damien. He quit a few months ago to concentrate on the Ripper murders. Apparently he's writing a book about them." Adamson's tone of voice made it clear what he thought of such ghoulish behavior. "He still does most of their coverage of the Ripper murders. We're just lucky he's kept quiet about the masks. Reporters aren't known for their cooperation with the police, but Damien's been decent enough so far. Now don't go getting paranoid about all this. We think the Ripper's got enough masks to keep him busy for quite a while—you said that last one you sold more than a year ago, so he must have been planning this for a while. Just keep your doors locked and your guard up."

"I do anyway. This is southern California, remember?" Lizzie said, with a delicate little shudder.

"How could I forget?" Adamson had said. "Give us a call if anything seems unusual."

Lizzie stared around her dimly lit apartment for a moment, willing herself not to imagine murderous shadows where none existed. She shouldn't have been so quick to turn down police protection. She shouldn't have been so quick to take Adamson's word for it that she was safe.

She flicked on the light, kicking off her sandals and crossing the rough wooden floor to stare at her ruined mask. She *was* safe, she reminded herself. No one knew who she was, presumably not even the Ripper. He simply had an affinity with her masks.

She shivered at the horrible thought, moving on into the kitchen area of the small, spare apartment and reaching for a bottle of fruit juice. She needed to get away from here. If only she had family, money, some kind of escape.

Her family was long gone, her father no more than a name on a birth certificate, her mother dead by the time Lizzie was in college. As for money, that had always been a scarce commodity, and working as a craftsperson in an overpopulated area like L.A. didn't lend itself to financial solvency.

Her friends, mostly actors, writers and the like, were even more impoverished than she was. None of them could lend her the money to get out of town, to go someplace where the sun shone without murderous winds ripping through your hair, a place where you could breathe, where you could meet a stranger's gaze and not have to worry about whether he was going to hit on you—or cut your throat.

No, for now she was trapped in her heat-soaked apartment. At least no one connected her with the Ripper murders. No one besides the police and that one reporter even knew about the masks.

Except, of course, the Ripper.

And even he didn't know where she lived. She sold her masks through shops and galleries, willingly paying the commission so that she wouldn't have to deal with the ugly financial details. No one had been asking about her; no one had tried to find her address. Detective Adamson believed she was safe from the Ripper, but she didn't share his certainty. If the Ripper ever found out where she lived, he would pay her a visit.

The ringing of the phone sliced through the shadows, making her jump and slosh the bottle of juice over her oversize white shirt. She didn't want to answer it. It was bad news; she just knew it. She wasn't ready to deal with any more disasters today.

The answering machine clicked on, quiet, efficient, spewing out her generic message. And then Courtland's arch, actressy voice, for once devoid of artifice, echoed throughout the apartment.

"You're in deep trouble, Lizzie, and you didn't even tell me!" she wailed. "It's all over the papers, and even if they didn't print your address, all anyone has to do is pick up a telephone book and—"

Lizzie had already snatched the receiver off the cradle. "What are you talking about?"

"You're there, are you? I should have known. I'm talking about the article in the *Chronicle*. About the Ripper," Courtland said. "And your masks. Why didn't you tell me?"

"It's in the paper?" The sense of doom that had been hovering beyond Lizzie's shoulders settled down with a heavy weight. "What does it say?"

"Everything. It even has an absolutely terrible picture of you. Like I said, Lizzie, you're in deep trouble. I don't know what the police were doing, letting that man print that article."

"What man?"

"His name's Damien. He's been running a regular column on the Ripper ever since the second murder. Haven't you been reading the *Chronicle*? I think you should sue him, Lizzie."

It was almost pitch-black outside. It wasn't that late, but the rain was coming down in an angry torrent. And somewhere out there, Jack the Ripper was waiting. Waiting for her. "Sue him, hell," she said, ignoring the tremor of fear in her own voice. "I'm going to kill him."

She slammed down the phone, then stared at her trembling hands. Why hadn't Adamson warned her? She didn't usually read the paper, and when she did, she avoided anything to do with murders in general, and the Ripper in particular.

He must have figured she was spooked enough, or maybe he hadn't known. The situation was macabre as it was, without the world at large knowing her grim connection to the grisly murders. She pushed her hands through her thick hair, forcing herself to take a deep, calming breath. Why did the Venice Ripper concentrate only on female prostitutes? Why couldn't he decide to pay a little visit to a man named Damien? Where was a good serial killer when you needed one?

She shook her head, trying to clear the morbid fantasy from her exhausted mind. Outside, she could hear the ever-present sound of the rain beating down on the two-story building she shared with a couple of starving actors. They were out of town, and she was alone. In the rain. With a killer on the loose. One who had a grotesque affinity with her.

She yanked out the telephone book and began leafing through it. There were more than a dozen Damians, none of them with the initials J. R., and she was about to slam the thing shut in frustration when she tried the alternative spelling. Only to find that a J. R. Damien lived within ten minutes of her house. In Venice. Where the Ripper prowled.

She punched the numbers into the telephone before she could think twice about it, but of course all of California communicated by answering machine, and one clicked on after the first ring. A man's voice, deep, harsh, cool, came over the line in a prerecorded message. Referring the caller to the *Los Angeles Chronicle*.

She slammed down the phone. It was the same Damien, all right. And there was no way she was going to get through the night without confronting him.

She sank down into the sofa, letting the waves of heat wash over her, and yet shivering. Why wasn't the constant heat warming, reassuring, comforting? Why did the very thickness of the sultry weather seem one more threat to her safety and well-being?

She closed her eyes for a moment. She hadn't been sleeping well. It was no wonder, of course, with a killer on the loose, a killer who had a bizarre connection to her. Even though she'd tried to avoid the gruesome details, some had slipped through, overheard standing in line at the grocery store, presented as a counterpoint to dinner when she was working her waitress shift. Those details would crop up in the middle of the night, as she lay in her narrow bed, and she would wake up in a panic, her body covered with sweat, the white sheets tangled around her like a shroud.

The house creaked. It was cheaply built, made to house the influx of labor after the war. The walls were thin, the foundation was cracked and sagging, the windows were loose in their frames. Jared and Frank were out of town—there was no one upstairs in their apartment, wandering around. Those weren't footsteps overhead. No one was nearby, lurking, watching her, waiting for the right moment.

She pushed herself off the couch in a sudden panic. She didn't want to check her doors and windows, making certain they were locked. To check them would be to admit that the fear existed, and to admit it was to give in to it.

She went through the motions. She ate a carton of raspberry yogurt, washed down with a fruit drink. She took a long, cool shower, dressing in an old pair of jeans and a faded tank top. She turned on the air conditioner, telling herself she should clear away the mess from the old mask, start a new one. A fairy princess, maybe. Or a political caricature. Maybe a wizard.

She stared at the ruined mask and knew she wasn't going to do any such thing. It was already late, and the heavy rain continued outside, slapping against her window, but she wasn't going to be sensible and stay put. Wasn't going to turn on the TV or curl up with a good book if she couldn't work. She was going out to find J. R. Damien and give him a piece of her mind. And then maybe she would be able to rest.

He knew who he was. The savior, the slasher, sent by God to wreak justice and revenge on the filth-ridden whores of Los Angeles. He'd come before, many, many times before, in different cities, different centuries, taken up residence in different mortal souls, but his mission had always been the same.

Sometimes they'd caught him. He'd been guillotined, hanged, drowned, shot. Other times he'd gotten away, his blood-lust slaked, leaving his host to live out a normal, peaceful life, with the memory of the bloody mission no more than a dream.

He came in many guises, and that was why they seldom caught him. That was why no one would catch him this time, unless he chose to let them. He became whoever he chose to be, his will so strong that people simply saw the image he projected, not the creature behind that illusion.

It was no wonder those idiot police couldn't find him. How could they find an executioner who was a derelict one day, a teenage boy the next? A linen-suited businessman, then a middle-aged mother?

He stared down at his hands, his clever surgeon's hands. He'd sent countless whores to their just reward—and it wouldn't be long before his mission was complete. And then he could rest, retire back into normalcy, complacency, no one ever realizing the great work he'd done. Just as before.

This time, he thought, he might like to be a woman. It was easier sneaking up on them when he became a woman. The sluts had gotten skittish, wary, and he had to become even more clever when he lured them to an alleyway. Fast with the knife, cutting off their screams before someone could come to their rescue.

He hadn't made a mistake yet. He wasn't about to start. But this time, he thought he would like to be a woman, meting out justice to her own kind. And as he watched his hands, she admired the bright red of her highly polished fingernails.

CHAPTER TWO

J. R. Damien leaned against the littered counter in his pocket-size kitchen, staring at the sagging cupboard doors without seeing them. The phone had been ringing all night—he'd stood there and listened as voices came through the answering machine, voices from his present, voices from his past, voices he could easily ignore. Just as he'd ignored the voice of his conscience.

Printing the article about the mask-maker had been an act of desperation. A despicable one—he knew that. The police had trusted him not to let out that particular piece of information, and Adamson had been calling on the half hour, fury vibrating in his cop's voice as he tore into him for endangering the woman. Damien had ignored the messages.

He'd had no choice. And he had no guilt. As long as the Ripper continued, more women would die. The police were a bunch of bumbling fools—Adamson was the smartest of the lot, but even he was too damned decent to get very far in his search for an unstoppable killer.

Damien understood the plain, unpalatable truth that he couldn't explain to anyone as matter-of-fact as Adamson. It was up to him to stop the Ripper. Up to him to catch him—in the act, if possible. Up to him to destroy him. And only him.

Because there was a very good chance that when he destroyed the Ripper, he would also destroy himself.

He slammed the cupboard door shut, but it bounced back open again with the kind of malicious contrariness Damien had grown used to. He wandered back out into the living room, wondering where amid the litter of paper and books and dirty dishes he'd left his cigarettes. He was smoking too much, and he didn't give a damn. As long as he smoked, his hands were busy. And he didn't have to worry about what his hands had been doing. Or to whom they'd been doing it.

It was the damned nightmares. He didn't believe in psychics, in shared memories, in any of hocus-pocus bull that was so popular in California nowadays. He was a pragmatist, a practical man who believed only in what he could see, hear, touch and smell.

But in his dreams, he could see death. He could hear the screams of the women before they died. He could touch death, could feel the sticky heat of blood, and he could smell it, all around him.

He knew things no one should know. There was no explanation, no *rational* explanation. Only one terrifying possibility that he wasn't ready to face.

He'd just found his cigarettes when he heard someone at the door. The bell hadn't worked for years, and he stood motionless, listening to the insistent pounding.

He moved slowly, barely opening the door a crack to stare out into the shadowed, dusty hallway. A strange woman stood there, and his sense of disappointment was almost overwhelming. From the moment he'd known someone was standing outside his apartment he'd had a bizarre feeling of destiny. The feeling that the answers to everything that had been tormenting him lay just beyond the heavy security door.

He'd thought, he'd hoped it would be the Ripper. But the woman standing there in the shadows was too small to be a killer. The man who'd butchered those prostitutes had an inordinate amount of strength, and there was no way a tall, slender creature like the one standing in his doorway could have wielded a postmortem knife so effectively.

He almost slammed the door shut. Almost. But something kept him from giving in to temptation. Curiosity, maybe. A sense of destiny. He stood, peering through the small crack in the doorway, and wondered whether she was going to be the answer to all the questions that had been tormenting him. He doubted it.

She shouldn't have come here. Lizzie's fury had lasted the ten minutes it took her aging Toyota to get to this derelict building, but it had begun to fade by the time she stepped inside the littered front hall. It wasn't locked, and the place looked as if it had only a handful of tenants. Damien was listed on the top floor, and she'd pressed the button. Nothing happened, so she pressed again.

She'd wanted to leave. It had been a stupid idea to come here in the first place, to storm into the night in a white-hot rage to confront a man who might very well be the killer himself. Alone at night, in the rain and darkness, she'd committed the unpardonably stupid act of exposing herself to someone who might be a monster. As the reality of the situation hit her panic fought to overtake her—but she refused to let it. Once she gave in to fear, it made her vulnerable, and there were all sorts of creatures who preyed on vulnerability, not the least of which was the Venice Ripper.

She wasn't going to see the Ripper, she reminded herself sternly, squashing down her uneasiness. She was going to confront the Los Angeles reporter who'd put her life in danger for the sake of his by-line, and she knew just what she'd find. Some cynical, middle-aged Lou Grant clone, with yuppie clothes and an attitude.

The elevator still worked, though it moved with agonizing slowness. And there was one lone light bulb in the hall. Whoever was peering out at her from behind that crack in the door wouldn't get a very good look at her.

"Who the hell are you?"

"Don't you know who I am?" she asked, in a voice vibrating with fury. "You ruin my life for the sake of your career, and you don't even bother to find out who it is you've destroyed?"

"Spare me the melodrama," the man said wearily. "As far as I know, I haven't ruined anybody's life for the last three hours. State your business and leave."

"I'm Elizabeth Stride," she said. "And since you were kind enough to furnish a serial killer with my name and photograph, not to mention a good inkling of my address, I think we could safely say that you've ruined my life."

"Hell," the man said. He hadn't bothered to slide the security chain on. He opened the door. "You might as well come in."

For a moment she didn't move, surveying him warily. She didn't know what she'd been expecting. Her images of a yuppie had vanished at the sight of the faded grandeur of his apartment. She'd been expecting some crusty, hard-drinking editor with a beer belly and a hangover. This man was the farthest thing from that cliché that she'd ever seen in her life.

He was too thin. His dark hair was too long—not trendy long, just shaggy and forgotten long. He needed a shave; he needed a decent meal; he needed two weeks of solid sleep. He looked at her out of those wary, haunted eyes and something inside her came achingly, painfully to life.

"You don't look like a Pulitzer prize-winning reporter," she said finally, stepping inside his apartment.

"Oh yeah?" he said, pushing the door closed behind her. "And what am I supposed to look like?"

"A yuppie," she said, looking around her with barely concealed fascination. His apartment was cluttered, shabby, bordering on derelict, with stacks of paper and dirty dishes everywhere. The place smelled like stale cigarette smoke, and rain, and despair, and she wanted to open the windows and let the night rain blow through. She didn't move.

"I'm downwardly mobile," he said, walking past her and flipping over some papers on his littered coffee table.

"I can tell. What is that?"

"None of your damned business. Trust me, you don't want to look," he said, flinging himself down on the sofa and stretching his long legs out in front of him. He gazed up at her, and there was a challenging look in his dark eyes. "As a matter of fact, they're police photos of the Ripper's latest victim. In color," he added, obviously relishing the effect his words would have on her.

She swallowed, trying to keep calm. "Why did you do it?" she asked, looking around the cluttered room for a place to sit. She finally settled on one of the least-occupied chairs, perching in front of a pile of books.

There was no mistaking the look of momentary horror on his face. "Do what?" he asked warily.

"Run that article. The police were trying to keep it quiet about the masks. Now they'll have a harder time separating the loonies from the real leads. They could have copycat killers. Damn it, my masks could turn up on every corpse on the West Coast!" Her voice rose to an anxious pitch.

"Don't flatter yourself," he said, reaching for his cigarettes, and she noticed with surprise that his long, elegant hands had a slight tremor. "You probably haven't made enough masks in your lifetime for the number of people murdered in L.A. every day. You've just got enough for the Ripper."

"And you."

It startled him. He followed her gaze to the two masks hanging on the wall. She'd noticed them the moment she'd walked in, with an eerie sense of recognition. They were two of her earlier ones, and two of her best. One was the face of a querulous old man, an oddly humorous mask that had always amused her. The other was a clown, with orange hair, bulbous nose, garish smile— and desperation in his curved cheeks. The fact that she approved of Damien's choices made her even more uneasy.

"So the Ripper and I have something in common," Damien said. "I'm trying to find out what else."

"What do you mean?"

"I mean I'm trying to find the Ripper. The police are doing a rotten job of it. The bodies pile up, and no one gets any closer to a solution. About the only person who's benefiting from all this is you. At least you've got a steady market for your masks."

She was going to hit him. He wouldn't have been able to blame her if she did—he'd deliberately egged her on.

She controlled herself with an effort. She was a physical person, given to hugs and extravagant gestures, but she had never been tempted to sock someone. Until now. "You're sick," she said, in a tight, angry voice.

"So they tell me. Listen, I'm sorry if I put you at risk. But I think you're a fool if you underestimate the killer. He's smart enough to know whose masks he was using. It wasn't a random choice. He knows who made those masks, and he knows who and where you are."

"Then why hasn't he bothered me?"

He shrugged, taking his time lighting his unfiltered cigarette, blowing the smoke in a steady stream directly at her. "Beats me. I said he was smart, I didn't say he was sane. My guess is, he's not particularly interested in you. You're not a prostitute, and your masks help him."

"But why *my* masks? Why not someone else's? I'm not the only mask-maker in the L.A. area."

He stared at her. "Well," he said measuredly, "they're nice masks."

"Stuff it," she said sharply. "I don't need compliments, I need the truth. You brought this out in the open for your own twisted reasons. You can damned well explain."

"My reasons aren't twisted. I want to find and stop the Ripper before he kills again. I'd consider that a fairly admirable purpose." His tone was wryly cynical, belying his own noble words. "And I imagine the reason he chose your masks, apart from their artistic merit, is your name."

"Lizzie?" she said, momentarily confused. "You think that means something."

"No, sweetheart." He was taking his time, and she couldn't rid herself of the notion that he was playing with her. He took another puff of the cigarette, delaying it. "The original Jack the Ripper murdered five women for sure, possibly more. Those women were ugly middle-aged prostitutes, while our boy prefers 'em younger and prettier. But the thought remains the same. Jack killed Annie Chapman, Catherine Eddowes, Polly Nichols and Mary Kelly. And a drunken forty-three-year-old prostitute named Elizabeth Stride."

She was going to throw up. It probably wouldn't disturb him, she thought—as a reporter he would have seen worse things. She swayed for a moment, and she wondered if she was going to do something as impossibly Victorian as fainting. He surged off the sagging couch, dropping his cigarette, and she felt those long, elegant hands on her, pushing her back down in the chair, shoving the books on the floor, pushing her head between her knees. "Take a deep breath," he ordered in a remote voice.

She struggled against his hand, but he kept it on the bare skin at the back of her neck, holding her down, and eventually she gave in. She could feel the warmth of his flesh on her cold, clammy skin, and a dangerous, answering heat filled her.

And then he moved, pulling away from her and disappearing into the kitchen. She leaned back in the chair, taking deep, calming breaths, telling herself she had no need to panic, no need to run. Wishing she believed it.

When he came back, he was carrying two tall glasses. He pressed one into her hand, ignoring her sound of protest. "Drink it," he ordered. "You need it."

She obeyed him, not interested in a battle. It was tequila, and she'd always hated tequila. But it burned, nicely, and calmed the racing of her heart. "Do you have any more nasty surprises?" she asked, in a rusty-sounding voice.

He sank down opposite her. "Not at the moment," he said. "For what it's worth, the police are aware of the similarity in your names. I imagine they didn't want to worry you by telling you."

"They think it's a coincidence?" She took another tentative sip of the tequila, watching as he tossed his back without so much as a shudder.

He shook his head. "They don't believe in coincidences. Neither do I."

She shivered. "At least you didn't put that in the article. I suppose I should be grateful you had that much restraint."

"Don't waste your emotions. It's in tomorrow's paper."

"What?"

"It's a two-part article. Tomorrow they're running pictures of your masks. Look at it this way—it'll be great publicity."

"Great publicity," she echoed numbly, taking another sip. "Do you want me to thank you?"

"You can double the asking price for your masks," he pointed out in an unconcerned voice. "At least you'll derive some benefit."

"It'll pay for my funeral," she said, draining the glass.

"He's not after you."

Her laughter was totally devoid of humor. "You don't think so? I'm glad you're so certain."

"Listen, if he wanted to kill you, he could have found you months ago. We're dealing with a very smart man. With luck, he has no interest in you other than your masks. As long as you keep making them, I don't think you'll be in any danger."

She just stared at him. "And what if you're wrong?"

He obviously hadn't considered that possibility. He looked across at her, staring for a moment, and whatever he saw was so horrifying that his face turned pale.

The glass shattered in his hand. He stared at her, unmoving, for a long, silent moment. "You were already in danger," he said flatly.

"Why? Because a madman likes my masks?" She could see something in his eyes, something that troubled her.

"That's only one reason," he said, rising from the sofa, brushing his hand against his jeans, brushing the shards of glass free. "For another, you're a single woman living in an area of the city that's been plagued by a serial killer."

"What makes you think I'm a single woman?" she countered, her eyes wary, as he advanced on her.

"I'm a reporter, Ms. Stride. I do my homework. You live on Sunrise Avenue, in an old white building you share with a couple of actors. You've lived there for almost three years, and in that time you've had two live-in companions, both for relatively short periods of time. The first was an actor named Freddy Peeples, better known as Franz Peters. The second was a struggling screenwriter whose name presently escapes me. You have lousy taste in men."

He was trying to intimidate her, with his presence, his knowledge, his nearness. But she wasn't easily cowed. "Maybe they have lousy taste in women," she shot back.

He glanced down at her body with a casual, sexual summing-up that should have been insulting. Obviously he didn't find her the slightest bit attractive. Obviously he recognized that others might. "I wouldn't say that," was all he said. "Suffice it to say, you live alone. You come out alone at night to visit a strange man who has a strong connection to the Ripper case, and I'm willing to bet you didn't even tell anyone where you were going."

She was no longer feeling defiant. She was beginning, just beginning, to feel scared. "I'm not that stupid," she said, cursing herself because she knew it wasn't true.

"Who did you tell?" He came up to her, leaning over her as she sat in the chair, and she scuttled back, trying to move away from him, but with his hands on either arm of the overstuffed old chair, she had no place to escape to.

"My friend Courtland. And I didn't tell her I was going to see you, I told her I was going to kill you," she shot back, still fighting. He was frightening her, and she sensed he was doing it on purpose. He wanted to scare the hell out of her.

"Even better," he said. "That way, if I'm caught, I can always say it was self-defense."

She didn't, couldn't, say a word, and he moved closer. "Don't you believe me?" he asked, and she stared up at him, mesmerized by his shadowed face, by the grim, lost beauty of him.

There was something about his eyes. Dark and tormented, they seemed to call to her across decades. She'd looked into those eyes long, long ago, in another lifetime, another world.

And then she moved, fast, ducking under his arm, scrambling away before he could reach out to stop her. "You don't scare me, Mr. Damien," she said, her voice shaking, as she stood silhouetted by the cracked window.

"Just Damien." He straightened up, not making any effort to stalk her. "And you lie, Lizzie. I scare you to death."

She didn't bother denying it. She took a deep breath in a vain effort to calm herself. "Is there any way you can stop the second part of the article from running?"

"Not even if I wanted to." There was no guilt in his voice, in his face, only a faint regret. "But I'll give you a piece of advice. Get out of town. Go someplace where it doesn't rain, where the streets don't run with blood. Go as far away from here as you can until this madman is caught. Until then, no one is safe. No one at all. And particularly not a maniac's personal mask-maker."

"I can't," she said, still staring at him.

"Then may God have mercy on your soul, Elizabeth Stride," he said. And his voice sounded centuries old.

She ran then, and he made no move to stop her. Out of his apartment. Down to the street, fumbling with the lock of her car, her hands shaking, terrified.

She drove too fast on the rain-slick streets. Her tires were practically bald, but she didn't care. She just wanted to get away from that haunted building, that haunted man, as fast as she could.

There were times when her own sheer single-minded stupidity astonished her. How could she have been so gullible, so trusting? To go storming up to that man's apartment, when for all she knew he could be the Ripper himself? She had to have some long-buried death wish.

Except that she didn't. She didn't want to die, she wanted to live. She wanted to do just what Damien had told her. She wanted to run away, from the murders, from the city. And from J. R. Damien.

Because once she'd looked into his dark, haunted eyes, she'd been lost.

He was right; she *was* crazy. Crazy to go to a stranger's apartment when a killer was roaming loose, crazy to look in a stranger's eyes and think she saw a glimpse of eternity.

Maybe what she saw was her own destiny.

She needed to get out of town. Tomorrow she was scheduled to work the late afternoon-early evening shift at the Pelican. She didn't want to, but she needed every penny she could earn. She had friends there, people who lived hand-to-mouth, as she did. But people who would help her.

She was going to do exactly what J. R. Damien had told her to do. Get the hell out of town. And try to get his haunted eyes out of her mind.

Damien watched her go, running out of his decrepit, shadowed apartment, slamming the heavy metal door behind her, running as if the Ripper himself were after her. He didn't move, just breathed in the lingering trace of her scent, the faint, flowery spice of her.

"Hell," he said beneath his breath, crossing to look out the cracked glass of the window.

It took her a nerve-rackingly long time to reach the rain-soaked street. Long enough that he almost went to check on her. The elevator in his building barely worked, and why should it? Of the twenty-four apartments in the run-down old place, only five were occupied, and his was the only one on an upper floor.

The streets were deserted as she headed for her car. It was an old Toyota, and in the dim light he couldn't make out the color. But he would know it again when he saw it. *If* he saw it.

He watched her drive away, too fast, and wondered if she would make it home safely. If he had any decency at all he would call Adamson and have him watch for her.

But Detective Finlay Adamson wasn't there half the time when Damien needed him, and he didn't like any of his subordinates. Besides, there was no reason to worry. Lizzie Stride was going to make it home safely. As far as he knew, she was going to be just fine.

And he was in a position to know.

He headed back to the kitchen, pouring himself another glass of tequila. Didn't they tell you never to drink alone? He couldn't think of a better reason *to* drink. To try to drown out the memory of Lizzie Stride's frightened eyes.

It wasn't his fault, he told himself as he tossed down a large swallow of his drink. Or maybe it was. But he was doing every damned thing possible to find out who and what the Ripper was, even if it meant endangering people like the woman who'd just had the sheer stupidity to come to his apartment in the dead of night when a killer was roaming loose.

The sight of her had disturbed him more than he wanted to admit. She certainly wasn't his kind of woman. He liked them sleek and sophisticated. She was an earth mother, stronger than she'd first appeared, with sleekly muscled arms revealed by the sleeveless tank top. Her jeans were old, faded, and too loose for his particular taste; her longish hair was a shapeless mass of reddish brown that was still wet from the incessant rain. She had wary, greenish eyes and a wide, generous mouth that had refused to smile. And no wonder. He hadn't felt like smiling, either.

He wondered whether she worked out, whether her entire body was as hard and muscled as her tanned arms. And then he remembered she was a mask-maker, working in papier-mâché and clay, and even stone and metal. She needed to be strong. And what the hell was he doing, thinking about the rest of her body, when he needed to concentrate on whether she might, after all, be the killer? Even the most insane possibilities had to be considered. Including the most unacceptable of all.

He didn't like her. Didn't like her narrow waist and the swell of her breasts beneath the tank top, didn't like her thick mane of hair, didn't like her mouth or her eyes or anything else about her.

But still, there was something about her, something that haunted him. She'd stood in his apartment, defiant, frightened, and he'd been able to smell the faint tang of soap and sweat on her skin, the rain in her hair, the tequila on her lips, and now he wondered what her lips would have tasted like if he'd crossed the remaining distance between them and kissed her. Would he have tasted life?

She had wonderful eyes. Huge, brown, full of warmth and a tremulous kind of wariness. Her eyes had held something else, as well. Filled with knowledge, and also doubt, they'd seemed to mirror decades of lost chances, a lifetime of faded dreams. He'd looked into her eyes, and for the first time in his memory he'd felt emotions, longings, impossibilities that had suddenly seemed possible.

As he leaned back against the countertop, his hip knocked a plate into the sink, where it shattered. He stared at it blindly. He'd made a vow, one he couldn't break now just because he felt a twinge, merely a twinge, mind you, of guilt. Of desire. He had sworn to do everything he could to find and destroy the Ripper. No matter who he was.

No matter if he turned out to be John Ripley Damien himself.

CHAPTER THREE

The old woman muttered under her breath, a steady litany of profanities as she stumbled through the rain-swept streets. Her ancient stockings sagged on her skinny calves; the shopping bags she carried dragged on the ground. She kept a sharp lookout from beneath her greasy tangle of gray hair. They were always trying to pick her up. All the do-gooders, trying to get her help, they said. A clean bed, a shower, decent food. Didn't they know she belonged on the streets? She could find all the food she needed in the overflowing garbage cans, and other treasures, besides. This was California; it was warm. She didn't need a bed and a blanket; she didn't need a shower; she didn't need medicine. She'd had enough of medicine in the years when her family had put her in that hospital. Once they'd let her out, put her in that halfway house, she'd stopped taking the pills. Hidden them, then thrown them out. She didn't need them. They stopped the voices in her head, the voices she needed to hear. The voices of God and the angels.

Telling her to kill the evil ones.

She glanced down into the contents of her shopping bag. The blood was beginning to soak through—she should have used plastic instead of paper. She chuckled to herself, then began to sing, a soft, off-key nursery rhyme.

Jack the Ripper's dead
And lying on his bed.
He cut his throat
With sunlight soap.
Jack the Ripper's dead.

Lizzie was late to work, deliberately so, rushing in at the last minute, her thick hair twisted up behind her head, her regulation black pants and white shirt damp from the rain as she sped through the kitchens at the Pink Pelican. She knew they were watching her. The television news teams had picked up Damien's articles, and everyone, *everyone,* knew of her connection to the ghastly murders.

"I didn't know if you were coming in today," Courtland said, watching her warily as Lizzie skidded up to the waitress station.

"Why shouldn't I? I need the money," she said, tying the white apron around her narrow waist.

"Not making enough with your masks, Lizzie?" Julianne, yet another aspiring actress, sidled up to her. "I thought you had a steady customer."

"Bitch," Courtland said promptly, before Lizzie could reply.

"Takes one to know one," Julianne said, with her customary lack of wit, swaying off toward a table filled with well-dressed customers.

The two women watched her go. "Damnation," Courtland said, pushing her own silver-blond hair away from her lovely face. "She always gets the best tables. Don't pay her any attention, Lizzie. She's just jealous."

"Jealous?" Lizzie echoed, aghast. "Of what?"

"You and the Ripper. You know this town—any publicity is good publicity. She'd give her right arm to have some connection to our local killer."

"She might just do that," Lizzie said, staring after Julianne's lush figure. Her three customers had turned to stare at Lizzie, fascination on their bland, handsome faces. "Oh, God, she must be telling them about me."

"Honey, your picture is in every newspaper and on every television channel in the Los Angeles area. There's no way you can be anonymous. If I were you, I'd go home and hide."

"I told you, I need the money. Courtland, I don't suppose you—"

"Flat broke, darling. I really wish I could help. For what it's worth, I don't sense that you're in any particular danger. I read your tarot last night, and I get the feeling you have a protector. Someone who'll watch over you, keep you safe."

"I hope you're right," Lizzie said, controlling the urge to glance over her shoulder. "I'm just not certain I want to stake my life on it."

Courtland put her perfectly manicured hand on her friend's arm. "You'll be safe, Lizzie. You trust me, don't you? There's death all around, but it doesn't extend to you. Why don't you come over tomorrow and I'll do a reading for you? You can see with your own eyes that you're going to be all right."

"I don't know enough about it. I'll just take your word for it," Lizzie said.

"Do that," Courtland said cheerfully. "In the meantime, you can take the next table."

Lizzie followed her gaze to two middle-aged ladies who probably wouldn't tip well. "You're all heart," she said wryly, and Courtland's laugh followed her.

Damien woke up with a hangover. Not from the tequila—he actually hadn't allowed himself to drink that much. From lack of sleep.

Since the nightmares had started, the vivid, horrifying visions that tormented him, he'd avoided sleep. Only when his body demanded rest would he catnap, usually for no more than an hour at a time, just enough to keep going. Just enough to keep the monsters at bay.

He didn't bother washing out the coffeepot before he started brewing fresh. He leaned against the counter, staring blearily at the slowly dripping black liquid, trying to jerk his brain into some kind of order. He had that feeling again. That horrible, lost feeling that something hideous had happened—and he could have stopped it.

He should have gotten used to it by now. It had started months ago, maybe even two years ago, long before the first Ripper murder. It had started the night Ashanti Mizrak, born Betty Brinston, had died. And he hadn't done anything to save her.

He waited until the pot held a couple of inches of coffee, then pulled the decanter away and poured himself a full mug, ignoring the sizzling steam as the coffee continued to splash down onto the burner. He didn't bother with milk or sugar—the sugar was full of ants, and the milk was rancid. He simply poured half of the scalding stuff down his throat, shuddering.

And then he remembered why he felt guilty.

This time it wasn't some phantom occurrence. Or even some remnant of deserved, leftover remorse. He had reason to regret his actions. He'd put an innocent woman in danger, and for the same damned reason. To get a story.

Not that Lizzie Stride hadn't been in danger already. He knew it, the police knew it, and she had to know it, too. She had too much clear intelligence shining out of her frightened, oddly familiar green eyes. Hell, he'd done her a favor, bringing it out in the open. Now she couldn't hide from the fact that she had an unholy connection with a crazed killer. And, despite her comparatively demure life-style, chances were that her time with the Ripper would come, sooner or later. Forewarned was forearmed.

"Hell, Damien," he said out loud, "you're a regular Mother Teresa. What other noble deeds do you have planned?" He drained his mug. When was he going to learn that he couldn't interfere with people's lives? Couldn't change them, couldn't change the world? Couldn't even stop one lonely madman from butchering women?

If only the dreams would leave him. If only he could sleep. But he wouldn't allow himself to, not until he knew the answer. Not until he found out whether the horrific visions that tormented his nights were the product of his overworked imagination.

Or his memory.

By quarter of seven that night, Lizzie Stride decided that she'd lived through the worst day of her life. Courtland had been right—everyone knew about her. Everyone stared at her, furtively, watching for something. No one wanted to get close to her, as if knowing her would somehow bring them into contact with the

Ripper himself. Hell, she thought with grim humor, it hadn't even improved her tips.

Her feet hurt. Her back hurt. Most of all, her head hurt, with a heavy, pressing weight, as if doom were hanging over her. It hadn't helped that the manager had kept an eagle eye on her during the afternoon shift, obviously taking note of her customers' reactions to her. Job security seemed about to be added to the list of her problems.

"You've got a customer," Courtland told her as she zipped past her on the way to the kitchens. "Third table by the window."

Lizzie glanced in that direction, but the booth was hidden by the Pelican's omnipresent ferns. "Poor and ugly, right?"

"Nope. Julianne and I made a beeline for him, but he asked for you. And he's kind of cute, if you like the lean and hungry look."

Lizzie took a step backward, sudden terror slicing through her. "I don't want..." she began in a harsh voice.

"It's not *him,* Lizzie," Courtland said, in a pragmatic tone of voice.

"How do you know?"

"I know these things, remember? Besides, the Venice Ripper wouldn't be that gorgeous. This guy just wants to talk to you. He's probably harmless—maybe a reporter or something."

She still didn't move. "What's he look like?"

"I told you. Gorgeous. A little haunted-looking, but then, I always liked the James Dean type."

"Damien," Lizzie said flatly.

"Is that what he looks like? I'm impressed. Why don't I tell him you've left? After all, I could use the

publicity just as much as Julianne can." Courtland was
already smoothing back her silver-blond hair in prepa-
ration for her latest conquest.

"You do that," Lizzie said, backing away. "I think
I'm overdue for a confrontation with Mr. Harkin. He's
been giving me the evil eye all day. I have a suspicion
I'm about to be fired."

"He wouldn't dare."

"Keep Damien busy. I'll slip out the back after I get
my walking papers."

It wasn't as bad as she'd thought. Mr. Harkin ex-
pressed his concern in low, doleful tones, made a firm
suggestion that she take a few weeks' leave of absence,
and paid her in full for her time that night. Giving her
a grand total of eighty-three dollars and sixty-three cents
in her purse. Including six dollars and forty-two cents
in tips, it was just about enough to get her as far away
as West Hollywood.

The rain had slackened by the time she stepped out
into the darkness, coming down in a liquid mist that
might have been refreshing. She moved to her old car
quickly, ducking her head, afraid to glance back at the
Pelican to see whether Courtland had managed to distract Damien.

She was just fumbling with the key when a hand shot
out and caught her arm, dragging her around.

The scream died in her throat as she looked up into
Damien's haunted eyes. "If I'd been the Ripper, I could
have cut your throat by now," he said.

She swallowed, hoping she looked nonchalant.
"Then I guess it's lucky for me that you're not," she
said.

"Don't you know better than to park in a back
alley?"

She glanced around her. There was no one in sight—if Damien wanted to do more than frighten her, there was no one to stop him, no one to witness him. "I'll take any parking space I can find," she said. "In an overcrowded place like this, you can't afford to be too choosy."

"You're a fool." His tone was bitter.

"Is that what you came out here to tell me?"

He just looked at her for a moment. The night before, she hadn't realized how tall he was. He was thin, almost to the point of gauntness, and that merely accentuated his height. His rain-spattered denim hung loosely on his spare body, and his long hair was pulled back behind his head. She looked up at him, telling herself that she didn't feel this irrational, emotional pull. Knowing she was lying.

"As a matter of fact," he said slowly, "it is. Among other things. I wanted to tell you I'm sorry I wrote that column about you. I should at least have warned Adamson. It's not as if the Ripper doesn't know who you are, but you didn't need the extra attention."

"No, I didn't," she said, still watching him. She got the feeling he wasn't the kind of man who apologized easily or often, and she wondered what had made him come out on a night like this to do it. "But you're right, it probably won't make any difference."

"He's going to come after you anyway."

A bolt of fear shot down her backbone. "Don't say that! You told me you thought I was safe...."

"No one's safe," he said flatly. "You're a smart woman. You know as well as I do that you're in danger, even if you're pretending you're safe. Sooner or later he's going to come after you. He probably thinks

you're his soul mate or something. Or maybe his ulti-
mate victim.''

"Stop it!" Her voice was shaking. "The police are
keeping an eye on—''

"The police are a bunch of incompetent idiots. The
only one with any brains is Finlay Adamson, and he's
not there half the time. They're not going to be able to
protect you any more than they've been able to protect
the eight women who've been murdered already.''

"Seven," Lizzie said.

"What?''

"Seven women. There've been seven women killed,
not eight," she said firmly.

"The number doesn't matter. What matters is that
you might be next.''

Lizzie leaned back against her car, feeling the dampness of the rain-wet metal soak through her loose white
shirt. "Do you have any suggestions?" she asked,
mildly enough, juggling the car keys in her hand. She
ought to jump in her car, lock it and drive away from
him as fast as she could. She was foolish to risk her life
on the basis of her instincts. Her instincts about men
had always been lousy.

And J. R. Damien was a man possessed. He burned
with an intensity that should frighten her, *did* frighten
her. But it couldn't frighten her away.

"I already told you—you should get out of town.''

"I don't have any money.''

"You have a car, don't you? A credit card?''

"No credit cards.''

"Then just get in this damned thing and keep driving till you run out of gas.''

The rain was coming down a little harder now, soaking her shoulders beneath the thin white shirt. Glisten-

ing in his dark hair. "That should get me approximately ten miles, Mr. Damien. Not enough to get out of the Ripper's reach."

"I'll give you money...." He was already reaching into his pocket when she held out her hand.

"No." Her voice was flat, implacable.

"Why not? You can figure I owe it to you. I'm the one who put you in danger...."

"I thought we agreed I was already in danger. I don't need your money, Mr. Damien. I can take care of myself." She didn't even stop to consider why she wouldn't take money from him. If she had any sense at all, she would take anything she could get, just to get the hell away from the city.

But she couldn't take it from him. He stared at her, frustration in his dark, haunted eyes. "I didn't figure you would. It's your funeral," he said flatly.

"Perhaps."

He didn't smile. "I'll drive you home."

"My car works fine."

"I'll wait and make sure."

She shrugged, deciding to humor him. She wanted to get away from him, away from the cocoon of warm, enveloping rain, away from the nearness of his body. J. R. Damien disturbed her, disturbed her deeply. And she was already troubled enough.

She slid into the front seat, closed and locked the door, and turned the key. And listened, with growing dread, as the car made nothing more than an empty, listless clicking sound.

Damien was standing there in the rain, watching her, no expression whatsoever on his face. She rolled down the window, looking at him in mute frustration.

"You look like you expected it not to work," she said.

"Are you accusing me of tampering with your car, Ms. Stride?" He seemed unmoved by the unspoken accusation. "Now why would I do that?"

She had no answer. She simply turned the key, pumping the gas pedal, hoping against hope that the damned thing would fire.

It didn't. With an angry sigh, she climbed back out, slamming the door behind her. She could always go back into the Pink Pelican and get a ride from Courtland, or, failing that, Julianne. It was the safe, logical thing to do. But there was something about Damien that didn't make her feel safe or logical.

"Did you offer me a ride home?" she asked.

His expression didn't change. She didn't know how she recognized the triumph that lurked beneath his enigmatic surface, but she did.

"Over there." He jerked his head toward a disreputable-looking sports car, one that had clearly seen better days, one that in someone's careful hands might have been a classic. In Damien's long, graceful fingers it was little more than a wreck.

The interior smelled of leather and cigarettes and rain. The seat belt didn't work, the seat itself was covered with piles of old papers and crumpled bags, and the dashboard was cracked and gouged.

"Nice car," she said.

"At least it starts in the rain." He didn't bother to look at her.

"It's been raining for almost three weeks now, nonstop, and I've never had trouble before tonight."

"Maybe it finally got wet enough."

She sat back, trying to find room for her feet on the littered floor as the engine roared to life. It was well tuned, despite the car's shabby looks. She'd known it was a mistake to accept a ride from him, but she didn't realize quite how much of one until she was trapped in the tiny little cockpit of the old British racing car with a man she found distinctly unnerving. Overwhelming. Frightening.

"I believe you know where I live," she said, in a neutral voice, staring straight ahead at the rain-soaked streets.

She could feel his eyes on her averted face. She didn't want to turn to face him. His eyes were too lost, too tormented. To look into them was to be sucked down into his torment.

"I know," he said, pulling out into the traffic.

The car had no radio or tape player—no surprise to Lizzie. He didn't strike her as a man who had room in his life for music. He didn't strike her as a man who had room in his life for much at all.

"Did you like the food?" she asked, looking for a neutral topic of conversation before the tension in the tiny car made her scream.

"What food?"

"At the Pelican," she said patiently.

"I didn't have anything but coffee. I didn't come to eat, I came looking for you."

"The food's very good there."

"I'm not interested in food."

"What are you interested in?"

"The Ripper." His tone was flat, vicious.

"Nothing else?"

"Nothing else."

"Then what are you doing here with me?" she asked, telling herself it was unadulterated relief that filled her as they neared her street.

"Trying to save your life."

"Part of your noble calling, Mr. Damien?"

"Just Damien." He glanced over at her, and his expression left her even more disturbed. "Let's just say I feel responsible."

The words hung heavily in the air for a moment. "I absolve you of your responsibility," she said abruptly. "I can take care of myself."

"Sure you can, sweetheart. Like parking in deserted alleys and accepting rides from strangers who know too damned much about the Ripper case. How do you know I didn't sabotage your car?"

"Did you?"

"You figure it out." He pulled up outside her white stucco building. "You got any security system here?"

"Locks on the doors."

He swore. "When do your neighbors get back?"

"How did you know they were gone?" she countered.

"I'm a reporter—it's my job to know things. Stay in the car while I check the place out."

"The hell I will." She got out of the car almost as quickly as he did. "I don't need your help, Damien. I can take care of myself, I told you—"

He ignored her, moving up the short flight of stairs to the front door, then coming to an abrupt halt. She barreled into him, and he caught her, his hands on her arms, strong hands, holding her there, and she could feel the intense heat of him, the fierce determination that rippled through him. She knew she had to be crazy not to run away. And she knew she was so crazy that she couldn't.

"What—?" she began, but he didn't release her. Instead, he shook his head, silencing her, nodding toward her front door. And she followed his gaze, and realized with a dull throb of horror that the door she'd locked so carefully now stood ajar in the evening rain.

CHAPTER FOUR

A moment later, Damien released her, stepping back. Lizzie could still feel the imprint of his hands on her arms, through the rain-damp white shirt, and she wanted to shiver in the sultry warmth.

"It's all right," Damien said. "He's gone."

She stared up at him in disbelief. "What do you mean, he's gone? You haven't checked. How do you even know it's a he in the first place?"

"I know," Damien said, moving past her into the apartment, flicking on the light switch beside the door.

Lizzie paused in the doorway, unwilling to be quite so trusting as she peered into the immaculate open spaces of her studio. She'd half expected to find the place trashed, but there was no sign of any recent visitor. She moved inside, carefully, closing the door behind her, shutting the rainy weather out. Shutting Damien inside. "It doesn't look as if anyone's been here," she said. "Nothing's been touched. Maybe the wind blew the door open."

He just glanced at her, his thin face derisive and disbelieving. "He was here," he said, stalking through the apartment with a kind of neurotic yet negligent grace. He paused, looking at her work space. "Are you always this neat?"

She followed his gaze. "I haven't cleaned for a while," she said defensively.

"You're a sick woman."

"I don't like squalor."

"Meaning I live in squalor?" Damien responded, and there was just the faintest trace of amusement on his thin mouth. "I couldn't live in a sterile operating room like this."

"Then it's a good thing we don't live together," she snapped, nettled.

He looked at her for a long, measuring moment. "A good thing," he echoed, turning back to stare at her walls. "Something's missing."

"Don't be ridiculous." She was getting truly irritated. Particularly since anger helped control the deep-seated tendrils of fear that were trying to fill her. "You've never been in this apartment before, and I happen to live here. Nothing's missing."

He didn't bother to respond, moving toward the rack she'd built to hold her masks while they dried. "He's taken a mask."

"Stop it," she snapped, as uneasiness began to swamp her. She crossed the room to his side. "No one was here, and none of the masks are missing. Don't you think I'd..." Her voice trailed off, and she bit her lip.

He didn't waste words. "Which one?"

She no longer tried to deny it. "The one I did last week. I called her *The Bag Lady*. She was actually rather sweet, with apple cheeks and a wrinkled kind of face. I must have taken it someplace, but..."

"He took it."

"But why?"

"Isn't it obvious?" Damien said wearily. "He must be planning to kill again."

Lizzie stared at him in horror. "Get out of here," she said in a low voice.

He didn't seem the slightest bit offended. He started toward the door, pausing to look at her. "You'd better tell Adamson. Not that you'll be able to reach him—he's never there when you need him. But you should at least make the effort. The Ripper killed two women one night, and no one's sure why. He might decide he needs another mask. And he'd come back here to get it."

"Stop it!" she cried. "You're scaring me."

He opened the door, and the night rain splashed inside, made dazzling by the light from the street. "I just want to save your life, Lizzie," he said. "If I have to terrify you to do it, then I will. Every woman in the greater Los Angeles area should be scared to death. You in particular."

A moment later, he closed the door behind him, and she was alone once more. She moved across the room, twisting the lock with angry force, then leaning her face against the cool white door. She could hear the throaty sound of his sports car as it drove away, and then there was nothing but the usual street noise.

"For someone who wants to save my life, mister," she muttered out loud, "you certainly are abandoning me easily enough."

She pushed herself away from the door, moving back to the row of masks along the wall. She couldn't believe *The Bag Lady* was gone and that absolutely nothing else was disturbed. Surely if the Ripper had broken into her apartment he would have been waiting for her?

Even assuming someone had actually broken in, who was to say it was him? There were hundreds, probably thousands, of thieves in this area of southern California. There was absolutely no reason to assume that the sneak thief, if there had been a sneak thief, would be the Venice Ripper.

Except for the fact that he'd chosen her apartment, of all places. And one of her masks was missing.

She traversed the spotless apartment slowly, looking for any sign of the intruder. There was absolutely nothing to suggest anyone had been there. Apart from the open door and the missing mask.

And how in God's name had he gotten in in the first place? Granted, she couldn't afford a state-of-the-art security system, but the locks on her apartment door and windows were serviceable. There should have been some sign of forced entry. Unless whoever had been there had the ability to walk through walls.

"Stop it," she said out loud, heading into the kitchen. There was nothing in her refrigerator but a jar of homemade granola, some outdated yogurt and a little fruit juice, and her stomach protested at the very sight. She needed something bland and starchy—comfort food—on a night like this. But all the meat loaf and pasta in the world wouldn't comfort her.

Damien was right, damn him, she discovered when she tried to phone. Adamson was out somewhere and couldn't be reached at the moment. And Lizzie wasn't about to entrust her irrational worries to an underling.

There were no betraying fingerprints lurking around the apartment, she knew that with an instinct that was irrational and unshakable. Whoever had come into her apartment was like a shadow, leaving no trace of his passing. Sooner or later she'd get in touch with Adamson, tell him about the missing mask. It wouldn't matter if it were tonight or tomorrow.

She wasn't about to talk to one of the other men on the case. Adamson knew her; Adamson had proof that her connection with the Ripper murders was only peripheral. But others weren't quite so certain.

She looked as if she had the strength to commit the crimes. She even had the knowledge of anatomy, due to the emergency training course she'd taken in college. She had no motive, but then, what reasonable motive could there be for such grisly crimes?

If they were going to suspect anyone, they should suspect Damien. He'd seemed to know her apartment had been broken into, he'd known that the thief was gone, that a mask was missing. There was no logical explanation unless he was the one who'd broken in.

But if it was him, why had he brought her home and then left her? Why hadn't he taken a knife to her, as well? Was it all some elaborate game of cat and mouse?

Her apartment was hot and muggy, and yet Lizzie felt chilled to the bone. She wanted a shower, and yet something stopped her. The thought that someone had been there, someone indescribably evil, made her skin crawl. She couldn't bring herself to strip off her clothes, despite the fact that she knew she was alone, knew the doors and windows were once again securely locked.

Against an intruder who'd had no trouble breaching them in the first place.

She found a woven cotton throw, one she'd bartered for with a fellow artisan, and wrapped it around her as she curled up on the couch. Usually she slept on the futon on the floor, but she felt too vulnerable lying down. Instead she huddled in the blanket, staring blindly at her row of masks.

She couldn't get him out of her mind. Damien, with the tormented eyes, the narrow, haunted face, the long, elegant hands. He was like some dark Gothic hero, a Heathcliff, driven by demons. But Heathcliff had been as much a villain as a hero, and he'd ended badly. Were

Damien's demons so strong that he would be beaten by them, as well?

He was fighting them; Lizzie could see that quite clearly. Fighting some kind of darkness, a darkness he called the Venice Ripper, but she couldn't help but wonder if there was more to it than that. The decaying apartment, the life on the raw edge of nerves, all suggested more than dedication to a career-making story. Besides, J. R. Damien had no need to make his career—his reputation was impressive enough.

He was obsessed with the Ripper. More so, unfortunately, than the police department. If Adamson had put a fraction of the same intensity into the case, the monster would have been behind bars long ago.

Intensity, that was the word for Damien. Intense, obsessed. Driven. And shockingly, disturbingly attractive.

She would be a fool to deny it, and she'd never been one to cultivate self-delusion. She found him attractive. She shouldn't. She thought she'd learned to keep away from men who were bad for her, but her previous relationships seemed models of sanity compared to her fascination for Damien.

It had to be the weather. Weeks and weeks of rain were enough to turn anyone's brain to mold and mildew. Combine that with the specter of a killer stalking the midnight streets of Venice, and it was no wonder she was feeling fanciful, irrational.

Vulnerable.

She should have taken his money. Pride be damned, she should have taken anything he'd been willing to give her, gotten in her car and driven to Nebraska or someplace equally midwestern and safe. She should have gone to find some nice, uncomplicated man, settle down and raise babies.

Except that she'd never had the wisdom to be attracted to nice, uncomplicated men. And she couldn't remember a time in her life when she'd been so drawn to another human being.

She snuggled down deeper into the soft blanket, closing her eyes. She could hear the rain beating against her windows, steady, soaking. She could hear the sound of traffic in the streets. Once she almost thought she recognized the distinctive sound of Damien's sports car. And then she fell asleep.

Damien wasn't particularly in the mood to be driving around in the rain. Neither was he in the mood to go home, alone, to the silence of his apartment. His mouth twisted in a smile as he thought about it. Squalor, she'd said.

Well, he liked his squalor. No, scratch that. He simply didn't notice it. He washed a dish if he needed it, took out the trash when he noticed bugs. Apart from that, he simply didn't care. He had more important things to worry about than being a good housekeeper.

Obviously Lizzie Stride didn't have enough to occupy her mind, which in itself was a surprise. She had a satisfying art; she had a job to make ends meet; she had an unnerving connection to a serial killer. Those things alone ought to make her concentrate on more important things than the waxy yellow buildup on her kitchen floors.

She needed a man. It was that simple. She needed someone to keep her so occupied that she wouldn't worry about dirty dishes and stray newspapers. She needed a man to carry her over to that futon he'd noticed lying in the corner of the room and tear the sheets off. She needed clothes strewn from one end of the apartment to the other, her clothes and his, until they wound up naked on that thin mattress....

"No," he said aloud, clamping a shutter down on his erotic fancies. Not him. She needed a man who could concentrate on her alone. She needed someone to make love to her, hard and often, someone to wipe that anxious look from her eyes. He wasn't that man.

Even if, for the first time since he could remember, he wished he was.

He pulled the Austin-Healey over to the sidewalk and parked. He could see her building from where he sat; he could see if anyone entered. If anyone skulked around the back, looking for a way to break in. He didn't really think that was going to happen, but couldn't simply go home and go to bed, assuming she would be safe.

He would watch. After all, he scarcely slept nowadays. He might as well spend the night sitting in his car, watching her apartment, rather than pacing the littered floor of his own squalid place.

He slid down in the cracked leather seat, staring at the building. The streets were almost deserted, only one of California's uncounted homeless wandering down the sidewalk, shopping bags in both hands, her skirts trailing around thick ankles. She had a filthy scarf over her grizzled gray hair, and she was singing something. He concentrated, trying to make out the words, but they were unintelligible, meaningless. It sounded like some old children's rhyme that he'd never heard.

She paused to glance up at Lizzie's building, and adrenaline shot through Damien's body. She moved on, muttering some old song about sunrise soap or some such thing. And then she disappeared into the night.

He forced himself to relax once more. The lights were still on in Lizzie's apartment, and he found himself wishing she had larger windows and no shades. He wanted to sit there and watch her undress, like the crudest voyeur. He wanted to enliven the long, endless hours after midnight with harmless erotic fantasies. About her soft mouth. Her long legs. Her muscled arms and that thick mop of red hair. In another lifetime there might have been the possibility—just the possibility, mind you—of something wonderful.

Her eyes hinted of that lifetime. Of a thousand lifetimes, all coming to a head in this one. He wanted to believe in that possibility, but he knew it would be a waste of time.

Right now there were no possibilities at all. Only staying alive for another day. And making sure no one else died.

She shuffled along the streets. Her shopping bags were heavy, but she didn't mind. She had the tools of her trade with her wherever she went, and she should be glad of the burden. She used the Giorgio bag for the mask. She wished she'd used plastic for the knives. Blood had a tendency to soak through paper.

No one bothered her. A lucky thing for them. They might think she was just a helpless old lady, crooning her meaningless songs. They might not see her power.

She knew where she would find her goal that night. She'd wanted to go back to the apartment, but it wasn't time yet. She had to wait until the perfect moment. Besides, that reporter was sitting in his car, watching her. She knew he didn't suspect, but he was busy watching the mask-maker's house. She would have to wait until later.

It was all right. She'd waited long enough. More than a hundred years, in fact. She could wait a few days longer.

In the meantime, she had work to do. And not much time to accomplish it. Humming softly, she shuffled off down the street, in search of the next victim.

Lizzie dreamed. Not of monsters or blood, not of masks and death. She dreamed of Damien.

Damien, with his long, elegant hands touching her, his fingers tracing random patterns on her hot skin as he watched her from his dark, haunted eyes. And then it was his mouth, brushing against her lips, his thin, mocking mouth, kissing her, pressing hard against her, so that she had no choice but to open her mouth and taste him, and he tasted of darkness and sex and obsession, everything she'd ever run from, and she kissed him back, willingly, reaching for him, wanting him.

His body was hard, hot, strong against hers, and his skin was smooth and vibrant. His hands were sliding beneath her clothing, beneath layers and layers, deft, impatient, and she arched up against him, reveling in the feel of him, the hunger he felt for her alone....

She was jarred awake, suddenly, rudely, and she was covered with a cold sweat, her hands shaking as she tried to summon back the disturbing dream. Somewhere in that dream were the answers, and they'd vanished, ripped away, just as her sleep had been, by the strident sound of the phone ringing.

She didn't want to answer it. She'd fallen asleep with the lights on, and she could see it was close to six in the morning. The sun was probably up already, but the rain was still falling. Another dreary day, and the phone could bring nothing but disaster.

She waited for her answering machine to click in, but the phone simply kept ringing, harsh, insistent, and she had no choice.

She knew it was Adamson before he spoke. She knew it was another death. And she knew what she had to ask.

"Do you need me to send a squad car?" Adamson asked, his voice solicitous. "It won't take long—we've gone through all this too many times."

"I can get there myself," she said wearily. "What mask was the girl wearing?"

"Does it matter?" Some of Adamson's patience was clearly wearing thin.

"Yes."

"I don't know what you'd call it. The mask looks like an old woman. Apple cheeks, gray hair. Sort of like..."

"Like a bag lady," Lizzie supplied wearily.

"Exactly. Is that important?"

"I'll tell you when I get there. Give me half an hour."

She got in the shower before she could think twice about it, then pulled on a baggy pair of jeans and a chambray shirt, twisting her wet hair in a loose knot at the back of her neck. It wasn't until she stepped out into the early-morning drizzle that she remembered her car had broken down.

She hesitated on her front walkway. And then she saw it, Damien's old sports car, parked a few yards down the street.

She walked over to it without hesitation. He was sitting in the driver's seat, asleep, his thin face shadowed with exhaustion. She almost hated to wake him up.

She moved around to the passenger side and opened the door, sliding in as he jerked awake.

"If you were watching over me," she said pleasantly enough, "then you aren't supposed to fall asleep."

He blinked, rubbing a hand across his stubbled jaw. The car smelled of wet leather and cigarettes, and the floor was littered with empty paper coffee cups, attesting to his long night.

"I just drifted off for a moment." He shifted in the seat to stare at her. "What's wrong?"

"I need a ride to the police station."

"There's been another murder."

"How'd you know?" she asked in an artificially bright voice. "And you'll never guess which mask the poor girl was wearing."

"The bag lady." He started the car with a savage twist of his wrist. "How come they didn't send a squad car?"

"They're getting used to this by now. It'll be the same old questions, and then I'll come back home."

"Not this time. He was in your apartment yesterday. They've got a lead. He might have left a fingerprint, a speck of dandruff. Something..." He pulled out into the empty postdawn street. "Didn't you tell them your apartment had been broken into?"

"I tried." She stared straight ahead, into the rainswept morning. "You were right, Adamson was out."

"They'd probably already found the body. Damn," he said, slamming his fist against the steering wheel. "Why the hell did I have to fall asleep?"

She turned to stare at him. "What's that got to do with anything?" she asked. "It didn't sound like the murder happened anywhere near us. You wouldn't have seen anything."

"No," he said shortly. "Of course not." But he didn't sound convinced.

The ride to the police station was short and silent. "I'm coming in with you," he said when he pulled up outside.

"There's no need...."

"There's every need. I was in your apartment last night. They'll want to talk to me, as well. I'll save them the trouble of looking for me. Besides, they might have found out something interesting."

"And you think they'd tell you? A reporter?"

"Adamson tells me things he wouldn't tell another reporter. Probably because I've found out things he hasn't. I have greater access to information. I can use bribes. There are street people who wouldn't think of talking to a cop, but who are more than happy to tell me what I need to know. We have a good working relationship, Adamson and I." His voice was cool and cynical.

"Then I suppose I can thank him for giving you the information about me," she said, making no effort to leave the car.

"No," Damien said, opening the car door. "I'm the one who told him about you."

Adamson looked up when they were ushered into his office, and his bluff face was blank with surprise. "Both of you?"

"I drove her here," Damien said.

Lizzie opened her mouth to correct the impression their arriving together must have made, but then she closed it again. It didn't matter to her what Adamson thought. It only mattered that he caught the killer.

"Take a seat," Adamson said after a moment's evident surprise. "I didn't think you two knew each other."

"I had to thank him for his newspaper article," Lizzie said in an acid voice. "It's not every day I'm made into a target for a killer."

"As you can see, this isn't exactly a friendly relationship," Damien murmured. "Someone broke into her apartment last night. The only thing missing was the bag lady mask."

Adamson started cursing. "Why the hell didn't you call—?"

"I did. You weren't here," Lizzie said. "For that matter, why didn't you tell me about my name?"

Adamson's eyes narrowed. "What about your name?"

"Apparently the original Jack the Ripper killed a woman named Elizabeth Stride."

"Coincidence," Adamson said staunchly.

"Don't give her that," Damien said. "She's a smart lady. She won't fall for it."

"All right. I didn't want to worry you."

"Don't you think I should have been warned?"

"He's made no effort to get to you. He's more interested in carving up prostitutes. We've been keeping an eye on you, just in case. As long as you keep making your masks, you're safe."

Damien snorted in obvious disbelief. "You don't believe that any more than I do. He's biding his time."

"Then why the hell did you put her in the newspaper, Damien?" Adamson shot back.

He didn't have the grace to look the slightest bit guilty. "Because I was sick of watching women die, while the police sat around drinking coffee and doing nothing about it. That article got things moving."

"It could have gotten Lizzie killed. Did you consider that?" Adamson said shrewdly.

"I considered it." Damien's voice was flat, dead. "I figured it was worth the risk."

"Who elected you God?"

"Stop arguing," Lizzie said sharply. "It's too late now to change things."

"I don't want you going back to the apartment, Ms. Stride," Adamson said, contenting himself with a glare in Damien's direction. "We're going to go over the place with a fine-tooth comb—if the Ripper left even a molecule of evidence, we'll find it. I can see about getting authorization to take you to a safe house, put a policewoman in your place as decoy..."

"No."

"You don't have any say in the matter."

"Wanna bet?" Damien drawled. "You can't commandeer her apartment without a court order, and if you do, I'll put it in my column just to make sure the Ripper doesn't make any mistakes."

"I could have you arrested for obstructing justice."

"Try it. I'm not going to sit around and let you set up some other woman to get killed."

"So what are your suggestions? Since you seem to think you're in charge of the investigation," Adamson said in a withering tone.

"I'm sure as hell finding out more than you are," Damien shot back. "Send Lizzie to a hotel, with a guard. Watch her place, but don't put anyone inside. He must have run out of masks. He only took one, and he's already used it. When he wants to kill again, he'll have to go back for more."

"We might find a fingerprint."

"Even if you do, you know you've got a snowball's chance in hell of finding out that this guy has a record," Damien shot back. "This isn't some career criminal. This is someone who looks and acts normal. A businessman. A lawyer. A cop. A reporter.''

"If you think you look and act normal," Lizzie said from her seat in the corner, "then you suffer from delusions.''

Damien turned to look at her, and she expected a glare. What she got was even worse. There was amusement in his usually bleak eyes, an involuntary curve to that thin, mocking mouth. Sometime in the past he'd smiled at her with just that dark amusement. She felt a treacherous warmth inside. Why couldn't she remember? And what in God's name would she do if he *really* smiled at her?

"I won't argue that," he said. "My point is, the Ripper isn't some weird character skulking in alleyways. He looks normal. He," he said, watching her out of those still, dark eyes, "or she."

It took a moment for her to understand his meaning. When she did, she was furious. "You know as well as I do that I was in my apartment all night long."

"I fell asleep."

"You think I'm the Ripper?"

"No. But I don't think anyone should be ruled out. Not even me," he said wearily.

She just stared at him for a moment, at his dark, haunted face. "Not even you," she agreed. Wondering exactly what it was that was haunting him. And why.

CHAPTER FIVE

"What do you mean, you can't do anything about it?" Damien demanded. "What does she have to do, be gutted on the front steps of the police station?"

"Keep your voice down!" Adamson snapped. "Do you want her to hear you? She's spooked enough as it is."

Damien looked through the smoked windows to the hallway beyond Adamson's office. Lizzie was sitting at one of the battered old desks, deep in conversation with one of Adamson's sergeants, and he had the chance to observe her without her realizing it. She looked tired, shadows beneath her warm brown eyes, lines around her soft mouth. She looked tense, wary, as well she ought to be. But she didn't look spooked.

"You underestimate her," Damien said. "She's handling this incredibly well. That doesn't mean she shouldn't be spooked. Sooner or later he's going to come for her. And unless you've got twenty-four-hour surveillance..."

"Ever hear of the financial crisis in the state of California?" Adamson asked him. "Don't you think I'd do it if I could? I asked, but there's no way. There just aren't the funds to pay for it. Too many women are in danger from this guy. We don't have the manpower to protect one lone female, even if she is connected to the case by those masks. After all, our guy's smart. He's not likely to break in again. He'll probably buy the next mask. We'll keep an eye on her, I promise. That's the best I can do."

"Not good enough," Damien said, moving away from the wall in sudden fury.

"What are you going to do?"

"Your job for you." He yanked open the door, and Lizzie looked up at him, her expression unguarded for a moment. It hit him like a fist in his gut. A complication that he simply didn't have time for. Feelings. Emotions. For her. For Lizzie.

"What are you going to do?" Adamson's voice followed him out of the office, repeating his question.

Damien ignored him, taking Lizzie's arm and pulling her to her feet. "We're getting out of here."

"I haven't finished—"

"We're getting out of here."

She came with him. He hadn't expected her to put up more than a token protest, and she didn't even bother with that. She walked beside him, out of the police station, no questions asked. She was a tall woman, but she still came up only to his shoulder. A strong woman, and yet he felt her vulnerability quite clearly. A beautiful woman, in a fierce, quiet way, and he wanted to stop in the middle of the corridor and pull her into his arms, thread his hands through her thick red hair and taste her mouth.

He kept his hand on her arm, possessively, steering her out of the building and down the front steps in the light drizzle.

"Where are we going?" she finally asked, as if their destination were no more than a vague concern to her.

"To a motel."

"Forget it," she snapped, yanking her arm away from him. "Just because I'm attracted to you doesn't mean I've lost my mind completely. I'm not going to a motel—"

"The police won't protect you," he told her, almost loath to interrupt her when her conversation was so artlessly fascinating. "Adamson can't get authorization, and you'd be a sitting duck in your apartment. I figure you'd prefer meeting the Ripper to living in my squalor, so I'm taking you to a motel where you can be anonymous and safe."

"Oh," she said, and there was a blush of color on her tanned cheeks. "I misunderstood."

"Not that I have any objections to having sex with you," he continued, beginning to enjoy himself. "It'll probably be pretty boring there, and making love is at least more interesting than the shopping channel."

"Go to hell, Damien," she muttered.

"So when did you decide you were attracted to me?"

"Go to hell, Damien." She started to charge ahead of him, but he caught her arm, and the light pressure of his hand stopped her short, so that she turned and looked into his eyes. For once he made no effort to shield his expression.

"Trust me, Lizzie," he murmured. "I've already been there."

How could she have said such a thing? Lizzie berated herself as she settled into the old car. Lack of sleep must have addled her brains. That, and a very reasonable fear. How could she have told a man like J. R. Damien that she was attracted to him? Particularly when it made no sense to her.

It was all part of that odd half dream, half memory. She'd known him, longed for him, in another life, perhaps. But not in this one.

If he mentioned it again, she would deny it, flatly. But for the time being she was probably safe. He was concentrating on his driving, concentrating on the cigarette he was smoking, and he barely seemed aware of her existence. She told herself she could lean back, relax, and she knew she was only fooling herself. There was no way she could relax as long as she was in his presence.

They drove along the freeway, leaving Venice behind in the murky daylight. Lizzie half expected the sun to start shining once they left the ocean, but the rain kept coming down in a steady drizzle. She leaned back in the seat, in the silence, and shut her eyes, exhaustion overtaking her. She woke up, staring up at him in confusion, when he put his hands on her.

"We're here," he said in a low voice. "I've already checked us in. You've been dead to the world."

She shivered. "Unpleasant way to put it. Where are we?"

"A small motel just outside of West Covina. The Ripper hasn't touched anyone outside of Venice. We'll be perfectly safe."

"We?"

"I'm staying with you. Don't get all starchy again, Princess," he drawled. "My only designs on your body are to keep it in one piece. Come on."

It was a seedy enough place, like something out of a second-rate movie, but at least it was clean. "There's only one bed," she said, eyeing it pointedly.

"You can count, too," he replied mockingly. "It was all they had. Don't worry, we can take turns. I don't usually sleep much."

"How long are we going to be here?" She pulled her gaze away from the bed.

"Until I can think of something better to do. With any luck, they found some evidence in your apartment."

"What makes you believe in luck?" she asked.

"I don't. Only bad luck. Why don't you lie down and take a nap, and I'll go see if I can find something for us to eat?"

"I'm not hungry."

"Neither am I."

He was standing too close to her. He was almost intimidatingly tall, but it wasn't his height that she found overwhelming. It was his intensity, his driven, fierce nature. He frightened her in ways she couldn't begin to understand.

"So tell me," he said, in a low, soft voice that was dangerously beguiling, "when did you decide you were attracted to me?"

"It was a joke," she said, knowing there was no way in hell he was going to believe her. He was too close, and his dark, haunted eyes could see too much.

A faint smile curved his mouth. "Very funny," he said. "We've already discussed the fact that you have lousy taste in men. You've been without a relationship for two years—and I'm hardly the man to change your mind."

She didn't know what to say at first, whether to scream at him for prying into her private affairs, or to assure him that she had no interest in either him or changing her mind. She went for the easier goal. "Who have you been talking to? Don't I have any secrets?"

"I doubt it," he said, moving away from her and dropping into a shabby modern chair. It creaked ominously beneath his weight, then held. "People love to talk to reporters. It gives them their fifteen minutes of fame. All I had to do was find the right people, ask the right questions, and your life was an open book."

"Not a very interesting one," she replied tightly.

"I wouldn't say that." He leaned back in the rickety chair, stretching his endless legs out in front of him. He was wearing the clothes he'd slept in—baggy, faded jeans, an old khaki shirt, running shoes that had seen far better days. The dark growth on his angular chin was moving past stubble and closer to bona fide beard, and his face was shadowed with exhaustion. "We'll go out for something to eat later."

"I'm not hungry," she said, watching him with unwilling fascination. He looked just about ready to collapse.

"You'll have to eat sooner or later," he said, his voice deep and sure. "If there's one thing I've learned during the last few months, it's that you have to make yourself eat. Otherwise you'll never keep going."

"You don't look as if you've eaten much," she observed.

"Enough," he said. "I'll go out for coffee in a couple of minutes. In the meantime..." He stopped, and Lizzie waited patiently for him to continue.

It took her a minute to realize he wasn't going to say anything more. He'd fallen sound asleep in the middle of his sentence.

She crossed the room and knelt beside him, staring up at him in quiet fascination. She wanted to take his long, elegant hand in hers, tug him awake and draw him over to the relative comfort of the bed. But she knew it would be a major mistake. Either he would stay awake, that burning intensity driving him still, or he would take her into the bed with him. And she wasn't ready for that.

The room was cool and damp, and there were no extra covers in the closet or the drawer. She pulled the chenille bedspread off and draped it carefully around him. He didn't move. She touched his forehead gently, her fingers brushing the long, thick hair that tumbled in his face. He didn't move.

She leaned over and brushed her lips across his mouth, so lightly that she could barely do more than feel his breath against her. And then she drew back, horrified at herself. And still he slept, unmoving.

It must be her own lack of sleep, she told herself, heading for the bed, kicking her shoes off as she went, that was making her do such crazy things. That, or the stress of the past few weeks, knowing of her unholy connection to a madman. It must be two years of celibacy, suddenly sending her hormones awry. There had to be some logical explanation for the insanity that had overtaken her the minute she walked into J. R. Damien's presence. Insanity, and a strong sense of destiny.

But at the moment she couldn't think of a single explanation that made sense. All she knew was that she wanted him to wake up, to put his hands and his mouth on her, and make her forget about masks, and murders, and endless rain. She wanted him to wipe everything out of her conscious mind except him.

She turned off the light beside the double bed, plunging the room into murky twilight. Outside, the rain was falling, but inside, they had to be safe. They were miles from the outskirts of Venice, and it was midday. For now, the Ripper had to be at rest.

And so would they.

Damien dreamed. It began pleasantly enough, and that was a rarity for him. Gentle hands touching him. Soft lips feathering against his own, and if he'd had even a fraction more energy, he would have kissed her back. Lizzie, he thought, knowing her taste. But he couldn't move, trapped in the mists of sleep, unable to do anything more than feel.

She moved away, and he was conscious of a deep, completely sexual regret. She'd knelt at his side before. He wanted her to pull the blanket away, to reach for his belt and unfasten it. He wanted her to put her mouth on him, to take away the torment and despair that had haunted him, leaving him with only the pulse-pounding need that could shatter into completion so easily.

But she moved away, leaving him hard, aching, unable even to open his eyes, to reach out and grab her. The rustling of the covers, the creaking of the bed, only increased his need, and he knew he could wake up if he wanted to. Could cross over to the bed and take her, whether she was willing or not. If she wasn't ready, he could make her so. He could lose himself in her body. Between her long, gorgeous legs, he could find a brief moment of forgetfulness.

He didn't dare. There were demons, monsters, surrounding them, a soul-devouring killer who could lay claim to them both if he forgot his mission. And he wasn't sure where that killer came from. From the rain-dark alleyways. From across the centuries. Or from inside his own twisted soul.

He sank a little deeper into sleep, the steady sound of her breathing irrationally soothing. He was back in a time when he'd had all the answers, back when nothing had mattered but the next story, the next award, the things that money could buy. Back when life had been simple and serenely hollow. Back before he'd lost his soul.

She didn't scream. He stared, helpless with fascination, as the flames licked upward, igniting her clothes, her long black hair, the haze of heat seeming to make her waver and melt in front of him. The flames spread to the now-empty gasoline can, and she was a human torch in the night, and she didn't scream.

He was the one who screamed. A harsh, rending sound, swallowed up in the night by the sound of police sirens and the noise of the crowd. He could have reached her, could have stopped the woman in her mad act of political defiance, and instead he'd waited a moment too long, for the sake of a story, a byline, one more prize, one more notch on his gun. He'd waited too long.

He could still smell it. Gasoline and burning flesh, melting hair and clothes and the plastic from her cheap shoes. It would stay with him forever, haunting him. The smell.

And the guilt.

The sky was red overhead. He didn't like to leave Venice. He was angry about that, and he would make her pay for it. He hadn't been in any hurry to finish with her. He'd been enjoying himself, enjoying the fear and panic that had spread through the city. Once he finished with her, his task would be complete. And he wasn't quite ready to stop.

But she might leave. Sooner or later he would find her, sooner or later she would have to come back to Los Angeles, but he wasn't sure he could wait. Things needed a certain orderliness, a certain attention to detail. If she left, if there were no more masks, then he would have to stop, his goal incomplete. He couldn't let that happen again.

It turned out to be a simple enough matter to find them. Enough people were watching for them, and the reporter's license plate number was well-known. It was on the police scanners—they'd stopped at a small motel in West Covina. Depending on the traffic, it wouldn't be more than a half-hour's drive from Venice.

He wasn't quite sure what he would do once he got there. He had a mask in the back of his car; the knives were cleaned and sharpened. He would have to get her alone.

He didn't want to touch Damien. Not in this lifetime. Not in the previous one. Letting him live, and remember, was reward enough. It was the reporter's destiny, just as Lizzie Stride was his, a second chance to make things right after so many decades, so many lifetimes.

No one would look twice at him. He was very ordinary today, middle-aged, middling height, an unremarkable face. He looked like a thousand other men in their cheap suits, heading home to a house in the suburbs. With only a brief stop on the way, not for a drink, not for hurried sex in the car with a twenty-five-dollar hooker. For death.

He pulled up outside the motel, waiting in the shadows across the street. He could be infinitely patient. Sooner or later one of them would emerge, and she would be unprotected. And he could finish what he'd started more than a hundred years ago.

He wondered what they were doing in there. He could imagine. Lewd, disgusting things, limbs entwined, mouths panting. Filth. It was no wonder the lights stayed off, even as the day darkened around him. If he moved closer, near the window, what kinds of sounds would he hear?

He gripped the steering wheel, his hands slippery with sweat, as his own breathing grew rapid and shallow. It was good. It was very good. The others, all the others, were soiled. He'd been unable to bring himself to touch Elizabeth Stride, no matter what his destiny proclaimed, because she was living a pure life. That purity protected her no longer.

He'd almost begun to wonder if she was different from the others. Better. He should have known. Women were diseased, creatures of filth, put on this earth, from the beginning of time, to destroy man. And Elizabeth Stride, despite her soft voice and warm eyes, was no exception.

It was after five when the white-painted door to room 13 opened. He held his breath, waiting. He'd hoped it would be Damien, leaving him the hotel room, so that he could take his time. But it was Elizabeth Stride, her red whore's hair hanging down her back, darting out into the rain.

She didn't look as if she'd spent the past few hours fornicating. But he couldn't let that deter him. The time was now, made for him, and he didn't dare hesitate. Reaching behind him, he picked up his leather briefcase in one well-manicured hand. The knives inside clanked together and then were silent as he started down the rain-wet streets, after his destiny.

* * *

Lizzie was absolutely starving. When she awoke in the darkened motel room, she was dizzy, disoriented and ravenous, and it took her a moment to get her bearings.

Damien slept on, slumped down in the chair, exhausted, not moving when she tiptoed around him to use the bathroom. The thin bedspread had slipped down around him, and she was tempted to pull it back up, tuck it around his long, angular body. She was smart enough not to. This time, after several hours of deep sleep, he might wake and touch her. He might take in drowsiness what he wouldn't want when he was wide-awake, and she shouldn't want him at all. As long as she could fight it, she could stay reasonably safe.

There had to be a place to eat nearby. Damien had been planning to go out for coffee; there was probably a convenience store, maybe even a fast-food restaurant, within walking distance. She would have sold her soul for a Big Mac.

She wasn't going to drive. He'd put the keys in his jeans pocket, and there was no way she was going to go fumbling around in his pants. If worse came to worst, maybe the motel office had a candy vending machine.

It was still raining when she stepped outside. They'd slept the day away; night had fallen, and she had the eerie sense that someone was watching her. Absurd, of course, the result of months of terror. The Venice Ripper stayed in Venice. He wouldn't be someplace as mundane as West Covina.

She started down the sidewalk, feeling the rain soak through her shirt. She paused at the corner, looking over her shoulder, but there were only a couple of people in sight. A bland middle-aged businessman type and a teenager. Neither of them looked like a serial killer— and both were intent on their own concerns. Dismissing them, she crossed the street, heading toward the busy intersection.

Damien woke with a start. The room was pitch-dark; from outside he could hear the beat of the rain, the whine of traffic. He knew without looking that he was alone in the room. That Lizzie was outside somewhere. Alone. With the Ripper nearby.

With a roar of frustration, he surged out of the chair, tossing the bedspread unseen on the floor as he leapt for the door. There was no sign of her in the parking lot, no sign of anyone. His heart was pounding in pure, instinctive panic. He was near; he was very near. And he was after Lizzie.

He paused for a second, trying to guess which direction she had gone, when he heard the cry. A small noise, almost a sigh. But he knew that sound, deep in his soul. It was the sound of death.

"Lizzie," he howled, racing across the parking lot in mindless panic, his feet skidding on the rain-slick pavement. He was blind with terror, unwilling to believe that it could have happened so fast, in one moment of inattention, that he could have gotten her, taken her, killed her....

He barreled into her before he realized what he was doing. She was coming around the corner, her arms wrapped around a paper bag, and he knocked against the woman, sending the bag flying. He almost pushed her out of the way before he realized it was Lizzie, staring up at him, in one piece.

"What the hell did you think you were doing?" he demanded, his voice harsh in the steady rain. "You could have been killed!"

She was looking pale, shocked by his fury. "He doesn't have any idea where we are...."

"He knows!" Damien shot back. "He knows everything! And he's here, damn it! He could have killed you!"

"You nearly scared me to death!" she snapped, bending down to gather the scattered contents of her bag. "I'm in more danger from you than any serial killer."

"Damn it!" He hauled her upright, fury fighting with the panic that had suffused his body and winning. She simply stared up at him, her face wet with rain, and then it was too late. He pulled her into his arms, shoving her against the brick wall behind her and kissed her.

Her reaction was immediate. She slid her arms around his waist, clinging to him as if her life depended on it, and kissed him back. She tasted of rain and fresh coffee; she tasted of love and hope and despair. He kissed her mouth, her nose, her eyelids; he kissed her throat as he threaded his fingers through her long, thick hair. Kissed her as he'd wanted to do for so very, very long. He wanted to rip open her shirt, to suckle her breasts; he wanted to drag her into the shadows and strip her clothes off her, to plunge his body into hers, hard and hot and heavy, taking her, possessing her, claiming her, until nothing remained, not him, not her, just sex, raw and hungry and life-affirming. Before he lost his only chance, as he had lost it so long before.

She moaned—it was a little sound of longing and despair—and he wondered briefly if he was hurting her.

And he didn't care. To be alive was to hurt, and for now she was alive, he was alive, and that was all that mattered.

He slid his hands down to cover her breasts, and they were full and hot against him, the peaks hard in the sultry rain, hard with desire. He wanted to put his mouth against them, and he yanked at the shirt, hearing the buttons pop and not giving a damn. No one could see them in the shadows, and even if they could, he no longer cared. His need for her wiped out his common sense, his judgment. All that mattered was that she was here, the rain-drenched warmth of her skin beneath his mouth, the swell of her breasts, the scent of her perfume, the sound of her choking little sighs. And he wondered what kind of noise she would make when . . .

The sound was a nightmare, slicing through his passion-haze. A police siren, screaming through the night, and then blue lights spearing the darkness. He jerked himself away from her, and he had the momentary sanity to realize that she released him reluctantly.

He stood a few feet back from her, trying to regulate his breathing, knowing there was nothing he could do to control the furious arousal of the rest of his body. If he touched her again, he would take her right there, in the alleyway, in the rain, with a murdered woman nearby and a killer on the loose. And nothing on earth would stop him.

She was leaning against the brick wall, staring at him, her eyes wide with shock. There was blood on her lip, and her shirt was open where he'd begun to rip it off her. She was wearing a lacy bra, one that fastened in the front. That detail burned itself into his brain.

"They must have found her," he said in a harsh voice.

"Found who?" She didn't sound any cooler.

He shook his head. "He's killed again. Nearby. I thought it was you."

"How do you know? It could be a burglary, a car accident . . ."

"I know," he said bleakly. "Let's get the hell out of here. We don't want Adamson showing up. He might find our presence in the area a bit too coincidental."

"Is it?"

"Is it what?"

"Coincidental?"

He stared at her for a moment. She looked unnaturally calm, watching him; he might have imagined the fierce hunger of her response. "What are you asking?"

"Did you kill her?"

He wanted to laugh. He knew that if he started he might not stop. "Stupid question," he said. "You'd be a fool to believe me."

"Did you kill her?"

He thought of his deep, dream-filled sleep, his sudden awakening. He looked down at his hands. There was no blood, no sign of anything. He looked up at her, and finally he was sick of lying, sick of being alone.

"I don't know."

He expected her to turn and run. He would have had to go after her if she did. He didn't know the answers, but somewhere out in the darkness a killer lurked. He couldn't risk having her find out the truth the hard way. If he was the Venice Ripper, at least she'd been safe so far. She would be much safer taking her chances with him.

"What do you mean by that?"

"I mean I don't remember. I was asleep in the chair—maybe I had a blackout. I've told you—I wouldn't rule anything out. Not even the possibility that I'm doing these things myself."

She just stared at him for a long moment. And then she knelt down again, gathering up the discarded food and wrapping it up with the ripped paper bag. "Let's go back," she said, in a quiet voice.

"Back where?"

"To the motel room. You need to eat."

"You trust me? Even when I'm not sure I trust myself?"

She looked at him, and then she smiled. It was a small, sad, wary smile. "You didn't kill anyone. I'll stake my life on it."

"You might be doing just that."

She nodded. "I'll take the chance."

And there was nothing he could say to that, nothing at all. But he knew that, if he didn't kill her, he would end up loving her.

And he didn't know which would be worse.

CHAPTER SIX

Lizzie half expected him to put up a fuss over her choice of food. She'd brought back fruit juice, trail mix and a packet of sunflower seeds. Damien ate it all, paying scant attention, his gaze riveted on the local television station. It didn't take long for the news bulletin, and through the narrow blinds they could see the flash of media vans, the lights flooding the area.

"The Venice Ripper has apparently struck again, for the first time killing outside the neighborhood of Venice, California. A prostitute was found in an alleyway in West Covina, her throat cut, her body mutilated. According to an earlier report by former *Los Angeles Chronicle* reporter J. R. Damien, the bodies have all been found wearing masks made by a resident of Venice named Elizabeth Stride. The police have refused to comment, and no word has been given as to whether the most recent victim was also wearing a mask. We're expecting an official statement in the near future."

"Damn you," Lizzie said wearily.

He ignored her, concentrating on the screen with his usual intensity. "He was looking for you," he said.

"How did he know I was here?"

Damien shook his head. "You don't think a murder in West Covina is a coincidence, do you?"

"No. I think . . ." Her voice trailed off as a heavy fist pounded on the door of the motel room.

"I bet it's Adamson," Damien said, shutting off the television.

He was right. "What the hell's going on here?" the policeman demanded, charging into the room and slamming the door behind him. He stood there glowering at the two of them, and he looked sane and normal and endearingly real. Lizzie wanted to throw her arms around him and hug him.

She controlled the impulse, staying on the bed, her legs curled up underneath her. "How did you know where we were?" she asked.

"I've had someone tailing you—and Damien, for that matter—for days now. We can't offer twenty-four-hour protection, but we can keep an eye on you. We figured you'd be safe here." He snorted. "We should have known no one is safe."

"Who else knew we were here?" Damien asked, his voice cool and low. "The cops, obviously. Who else?"

"Probably anyone who has a scanner. Anyone else who might have been watching you. Did you call anyone, let anyone know where to find you?"

"Do I look like an idiot?" Damien snapped.

Guilt swamped Lizzie. It had only been one small phone call, surely harmless. "I called someone," she admitted, in a small voice.

Both men turned to glare at her. "Why the hell did you do that?" Damien demanded, and he might have been a completely different man from the one who'd caught her in the rain and kissed her with such desperation. Might have been, except that her mouth still felt bruised and tender, her stomach knotted in memory, and her breasts tingled, just from looking at him.

"I wanted to tell my friend Courtland where I was. She tends to worry about me."

"With good reason," Adamson said. He was looking old that night, his thinning gray hair flyaway, his deep, basset-hound eyes mournful. "Better give me her name and address and I'll have her checked out."

"Don't be ridiculous, Courtland wouldn't hurt a fly," Lizzie protested.

"Listen, Ms. Stride, we don't have that many choices. Admittedly, it could have been someone from the department, with access to police information, but I'm not about to believe that unless I've got ironclad proof. He must have found out some other way. And I damned well intend to find out how that happened."

"Your department isn't looking any too good with this investigation, Adamson," Damien said.

"Do you think I care about that? First and foremost, I want to stop this creep. I'll worry about job security later." He ran a hand through his thinning hair, obviously harassed. "You two staying here?"

"No," Damien said, before Lizzie could answer.

"Don't leave the state. As a matter of fact, don't even leave the city limits. We can't protect you if you do, and if you disappear, so will our only lead."

"She's not going to be a sitting duck for a madman," Damien said sharply.

"Are you sure you mean that? You want to catch this guy just as much as we do. Think of your book sales. That's why you're hanging around her, isn't it? You didn't have any qualms about printing her name in the papers. You aren't worried about saving her life, you just want to be in at the kill."

Damien lunged for him. It happened so fast that Lizzie was still sitting there, watching in astonishment, as Damien's fist slammed into Adamson's jaw, throwing him back against the open door. And then she was off the bed, grabbing hold of Damien, pulling him away.

He went willingly enough; otherwise, Lizzie's strength would have been no match for him. Adamson was rubbing his jaw, and his eyes were dark with dislike. "I could have you thrown in jail for that," he said.

"And my publishers would get me out just as quickly," Damien taunted in a rough voice. "Besides, you need me to do your job for you. You can't keep Lizzie safe. I can."

"Can you?"

"I can do a hell of a lot better job than you can," he snapped.

"Don't think you can leave the area," Adamson said. "If you do, my men will find you and drag you back."

"At least she'd get some police protection."

"Stop talking about me as if I'm not here," Lizzie said sharply. "I can take care of myself. I don't need Damien or the police watching out for me."

The two men stared at her in disbelief, plainly united for once. Then Damien spoke. "We won't leave. Not as long as I think she's got as good a chance here as anywhere. At least here I can watch out for her."

"Don't you think that's the department's job?" Adamson demanded. "What makes you think you can do any better than we can?"

"The police haven't inspired me with much confidence lately," Damien drawled. "I prefer to rely on myself."

"I think we can do as good a job as anyone. This guy isn't real, Damien." Adamson's voice was shaken, unguarded. "He's murdered women, cut them apart with supernatural speed, and no one has seen or heard a thing. He's not human. He has powers—"

"Stop it!" Lizzie said, her voice hoarse with strain. Damien was watching her, his eyes dark and haunted.

"You're right," Adamson said, shaking his head. "I'm letting it get to me. We'll catch him, Ms. Stride. We'll get the bastard, if it's the last thing I do." He headed for the door, but Damien's cool, cynical voice stopped him.

"I take it you aren't going to press charges? Assaulting an officer and all that?"

Adamson managed a faint grin. "I guess this time I might have had it coming. Just don't let it happen again, Damien. I might not be in such a cheery mood." And he slammed the door behind him, leaving the two of them alone once more.

Damien wouldn't meet her gaze. He went back to the television, switching it on in time to see Adamson himself on tape. "We're looking into all possibilities, but at this point we tend to think this is a case of a copycat killer. The Venice Ripper has never been known to stray away from Venice, and there is no reason to assume he'd pick West Covina."

"Damn him," Damien muttered, throwing himself back into his chair.

"He doesn't really believe that, does he?"

"Of course not. He's just feeding the public more lies." Damien ran a hand through his long, thick hair and shut his eyes. "He's right about one thing, though. The Ripper will find you. If he wants to. There's no safe place to hide."

Lizzie shivered. "What do you suggest I do? Stake myself out on the corner of Hollywood and Vine and wait for him to come and cut my throat?"

"He does more than that," Damien said.

She fought back her sudden horror. "Stop it." She straightened, suddenly knowing what she needed. "I want to go home."

"Where? Back to Michigan?"

She didn't even bother to ask how he knew where she came from. Damien seemed to know everything. "To my apartment," she said.

"Why? He knows where you live."

"He probably knows where you live, as well," she pointed out. "He seems to know everything."

"Don't listen to Adamson. We're not dealing with a supernatural force here. He's a killer, plain and simple. A human being, twisted, but very real."

"I want to go back to my apartment," she said. "And then I want to go out shopping. You can come with me if you want, or you can go back to your own squalor."

"Oh, I think I'm willing to try your squalor for a change," he drawled. "Why the hell do you want to go shopping? What is it you have a sudden need for?"

"My masks," she said flatly.

He'd almost had her. He'd reached out his hands for her, ready to pull her back into the alleyway, and then he'd known he couldn't. Whatever she'd been doing in that motel room, it hadn't been what he'd thought. She hadn't been touched, hadn't been doing filthy things with the reporter. He'd known it with a miserable certainty. And he'd known that he couldn't kill her.

The rules were very simple, and very strict. He had to punish them, punish them all, ending with Long Liz Stride. But they had to carry a man's mark on their body, proof of their wicked ways. They had to die, fresh from the act of fornication, as penance for leading men away from their God-given duty. They had to die in a state of sin. If they didn't, all his plans would be for nothing.

Why hadn't she been with Damien? He'd seen them together, watched them from a distance. He could see the power between them, that sick, wicked desire that was eating them up. Why hadn't they given in to it?

He wouldn't accept the possibility that she knew better. She was for him. It was for her that he'd come back, to finish what he'd started. She wouldn't cheat him again.

No one looked at him as he walked down the street, shuffling, stinking of months of accumulated filth. Of all the people he became, he liked the street people the best. No one ever looked them in the eye, no one came close to them. Except for that one softhearted whore, who'd given him a five-dollar bill as he'd shuffled by, two weeks ago. He still had her kidney in his refrigerator.

His hands were trembling. He couldn't wait much longer for Long Liz Stride. His time, his destiny, was running out. The red sky would turn to blue, the rain would stop, and the Venice Ripper would be no more, would be returned to his safe life. Three more days. He felt it in his aching bones.

He had to hurry.

God, why had he kissed her? Damien was berating himself. If it had been up to him, he would have taken her in the alleyway, ripped off her clothes and had her, there and then. He'd forgotten when he'd last had sex— it was one of those primal bodily urges that he'd been ignoring, like the need for food and sleep. He'd given in to the other two when deprivation overwhelmed him.

Maybe it was as simple as that. Too long without a woman, and you were all over the first one who held still long enough for you to nail her.

Except he knew that wasn't true. There were any number of women who would hold still for him, always had been, always would be. He was considered an attractive man, and his cool remoteness had the paradoxical affect of making women want him even more. He was used to being able to pick and choose, if he wanted to, but recently he just hadn't wanted to.

Until Lizzie Stride had come storming into his apartment, chest heaving, brown eyes glaring, thick red hair coming undone down her back. Suddenly there was something more in his bleak life than his obsession with the Ripper. Something he didn't want to make room for. Something that barged right in and took up residence in what passed for his conscience, his soul. His heart.

He knew her. Was drawn to her through the dark, swirling tunnel of an endless past. He knew her mouth, the taste and feel of it achingly familiar. But he didn't know her body. Never had he lost himself in the sweet, warm strength of her arms. Never had he listened to her cry out in pleasure as she clutched him tightly.

He forced his thoughts away from that mesmerizing fantasy. One thing was undeniable. She was the only person in months who'd made him smile. The only person who'd gotten past his obsession, past the defenses and the wall of determination he'd built around himself. He didn't like it. He didn't like her. Didn't like her soft mouth and her rich red hair, didn't like her breasts and her hips and her waist. The scent of her, the feel and taste of her, the wry, unexpected humor of her. And most of all he didn't like her eyes, and the lost lives he could see reflected in their rich, warm depths.

She was a complication so complete he wasn't sure he could handle it. But the alternative was impossible, as well. He couldn't abandon her to her own devices. If he did, he would be abandoning her to the Ripper. And he bore his own culpability for writing that article. He had to save her.

There was always the remote possibility that the current Ripper knew nothing about his bloody predecessor, and that Lizzie's name was nothing more than an eerie coincidence. That his choice of her masks was random.

And you might as well throw in Santa Claus and the tooth fairy while you're at it, he thought bitterly. The Venice Ripper knew exactly what he was doing. And no one knew enough to stop him.

The search for Lizzie's masks was a revelation. She tended not to sell her work through upscale galleries, and they were far more modestly priced than they deserved to be. He wondered how she could survive in the high-priced atmosphere of southern California. Not that it was any of his concern. But it explained why she didn't even have enough money for gas to get her out of town.

The masks tended to be displayed in small hole-in-the-wall craft shops, places that reeked of incense and oil and people who lived on garlic. They were jumbled in among the New Age books, the overpriced crystals, the bottles of scented oil and the arcane instruments that surely had their uses, though he couldn't imagine what. The first two stores they tried had sold their masks weeks ago, and each one had had a different purchaser. It wasn't until they stopped outside a particularly dark and dank little shop near the freeway that she turned to him. "I'm going to need some money," she said stiffly.

It amused him. "I've already offered you..."

"I'm sure Hickory still has one of my masks, and he's already paid me for it. I needed an advance, and he was kind enough to give it to me. He's a saint, and he'd give me the mask back without money if I asked for it, but I'm not. I'm going to pay him."

"How much?" Damien reached into his wallet.

"It was an expensive one. Hickory insisted on paying me more than it was worth, and I wasn't in a position to argue."

"How much?"

"A hundred dollars."

He didn't even blink. He peeled off some rumpled twenties and handed them to her, then opened the car door.

"You don't need to come in," she said hurriedly.

"I'm coming." He slammed the car door behind him, looking around at the busy sidewalks. It was getting late, after nine, and the hookers were out in force. They'd taken to traveling in pairs since the Ripper murders, but even that hadn't proven much protection. Most customers weren't willing to pay for two, and only a few of them enjoyed an audience.

Hickory's Mystic Wonders was three doors down from a strip joint, and across the street from a burger place. Venice never failed to amaze him, Damien thought.

"I don't want you to insult him," Lizzie said hurriedly, running to keep up with him. "Hickory has amazing...gifts, and he has no qualms about using them. I don't want you to hurt his feelings."

He glanced down at her with hooded eyes. "I promise I'll behave myself. As long as he doesn't insist on telling my fortune."

Lizzie made a face. "He might," she admitted, and preceded him into the shop.

"I knew you were coming, Little Flame," an elderly voice said, drifting from the back of the store on a wave of incense.

"Little Flame?" Damien muttered under his breath.

"Shut up, Damien," she hissed. She plastered a beatific smile on her face as an old man hobbled toward them. "Hickory," she said, flinging her arms around his bent figure, and for a moment Damien felt an irrational flash of jealousy. Not for the man, per se, but for Lizzie's wholehearted affection, freely given.

Not that he wanted it, he warned himself. He'd done everything he could to keep her at arm's length. Well, almost everything, he amended, up until the time he'd been fool enough to kiss her. But just once he would like someone to look at him with such innocent, compelling affection.

No, that was a lie. He didn't want someone. He wanted *Lizzie* to look at him like that.

"Hickory, I need to buy my mask back from you," she said in an urgent voice. "I've got the money...."

"Much as it distresses me, dear one, I no longer have it. A man came in to buy it just this morning. I didn't wish to sell it to him, so I named an impossible price, but he bought it anyway. I owe you the balance."

Lizzie's shoulders sank in defeat. "That's all right, Hickory. You bought it from me. You're entitled to make a profit—after all, it's your business."

"But not a profit such as this." He shambled over to the littered counter and reached under to pull out a faded cloth sack. From it he withdrew three hundred-dollar bills and handed them to a shocked Lizzie.

"Not the safest way to keep your money, old man," Damien said in a caustic voice.

Those ageless, milky blue eyes focused on him for a moment. "You brought him here," he said. "You found him, after all this time. You must care about him."

"Not particularly," Lizzie said, in a dry voice. "And I only just met him."

"This time around," he said obscurely. "You can't fool me, Little Flame," Hickory murmured, touching Lizzie's hair with a gentle gesture, and Damien found himself wanting to knock the old man's hand away. "This man means a great deal to you." He came closer, and Damien held his ground, staring down at him with all his ironclad defenses in place. "Who is he?"

"He's a friend of mine, Hickory. Sort of. His name is Damien."

"The reporter," Hickory said, in a knowing voice. He reached out and put his withered hand on Damien's arm, and it was all Damien could do not to jerk away. He felt something that was uncannily like a strong electric current from the man's skin, one that pulsed and flowed. "You are wrong," he said, looking up into Damien's eyes. "You worry needlessly."

"Oh, yeah?" he drawled. "Tell me about it."

"I would be more than happy to," he answered seriously. "But you are far from ready to listen. Your ears are full of your own fear and anger, and until wisdom unstops them, what I say will be meaningless."

"I'm not going to argue with that one."

"Damien!" Lizzie breathed, shocked at his rudeness.

But Hickory simply nodded, unoffended. "He will know when it is time, mask-maker. When he wishes to hear the truth, bring him back to me. Then I will tell you both of the past, of the future. The present is not as clear. In the meantime, take care of him."

"It's supposed to be the other way around," Lizzie muttered.

Hickory's smile was beatific. "It's always best when it goes both ways. Blessings upon you both."

She waited until they were back outside. The streets of Venice were even more raucous than usual, loud music blaring forth from a neighborhood bar. She caught his arm as he started around to the driver's side of the Austin-Healey and he could feel her fury.

"I told you not to do that."

"The old man can take care of himself," he replied.

"You were nasty."

"I was honest."

"So was he. He only wanted to help."

"Let him help someone who's a little more gullible," Damien snapped, more unsettled by the encounter than he wanted to admit. "Past lives. I've never heard such crap."

"He's right. You're hopeless."

"He didn't say that," Damien reminded her, prompted by some perverse streak. "He just said I wasn't ready. You're supposed to take care of me until I am."

"I'd like to take care of you, all right," she snarled.

"How many more stops?"

It startled her out of her rage. "I beg your pardon?"

"How many more hocus-pocus convenience stores do we drop by? Who else has your masks?"

"No one," she said, her anger leaving her like a deflated balloon. "Those were the last three places where I thought they might still have a few. At least I can be sure the Ripper didn't buy them, even if he may have ended up with them."

"What makes you say that?"

"Didn't you hear? At The Ruby Tiger the mask was bought by a teenage boy. At The Water's Edge it was bought by a young woman. This one was bought by a businessman. They can't be the same person. The Ripper is one person, not three."

"I wouldn't count on that, Lizzie. I wouldn't count on a damned thing where the Ripper's concerned," he said dourly. "Do you know how many of those masks have been used yet?"

"I'm not certain, but I think two of them. I'm afraid I've never paid much attention to where I place my masks. Each store takes two or three, and eventually they pay me. I don't know which ones end up where."

"Damned stupid way to run a business."

"It's not a business, it's an art," she shot back.

"It's murder, Lizzie."

"Stop it, Damien!" Her voice was strained, and she controlled herself with an effort. "He used one on the girl in West Covina, according to the television reporter." She looked out into the milling crowd. "That doesn't mean he's out of masks. I thought he might have been, but I can't be sure that all of the ones I've made over the years have been accounted for."

"So he can just keep going. Damn it." He slammed his fist down on the low hood of the Austin-Healey, making a dent. "Get in the car, Lizzie."

"Where are we going?"

"That's up to you. You've got enough money for a plane ticket now, without having to accept my filthy lucre."

"Take me home," she said. "To my apartment."

"Are you going to let me come, too? I'm not in the mood for another night in the front seat of this car. My legs are too long."

She glanced down at his legs, and there was a startled, sexual awareness in her eyes. One she quickly shuttered.

"You could go home," she said coolly.

"I'm not leaving you. There are too many questions left. And I can't get rid of the feeling that you hold the answers."

"I'm not keeping anything from you."

"Not consciously. Face it, Lizzie, I'm not leaving you. I'm your only chance at staying alive, and I intend to watch over you."

"A protector," she murmured, looking both startled and relieved. "Courtland told me someone would show up to do just that."

"I can't do it from the front seat of my car," he said. "Let me come home with you."

"If you behave yourself," she said, opening the door and sliding in.

Over the dented roof of his car, he could see the hookers parading down the street, and beyond the feathered and beshawled window of Hickory's store he could see the old man looking out at them. "Behave myself, hell," Damien muttered. And he slid behind the wheel.

CHAPTER SEVEN

Lizzie's apartment smelled stale and musty. If the police were still watching the place, there was no sign of them when she unlocked the front door, and it took all her self-control not to flinch when she pushed it open. She wasn't sure what she expected to find, but knowing Damien was standing directly behind her, tall and strong and infinitely infuriating, was some measure of comfort.

She flicked on the overhead lights, and her gaze went immediately, anxiously, to the far wall. All her masks were still in place, not a single one taken. She felt relief course through her, coupled with an irrational feeling of guilt. Her part in this whole ghastly mess wasn't finished yet.

She watched as Damien prowled the apartment, checking the windows, the doors, poking into her refrigerator and her cupboards. She stood in the middle of the room, watching him. "Are you hungry? I can fix something...."

"No," he said, closing the kitchen cabinet. "Where do you keep your liquor?"

"I don't."

He just looked at her for a moment. "Nothing? Not a bottle of beer, a few inches of Scotch, some wine on its way to becoming vinegar? Hell, cooking sherry will do."

"I thought you were here to protect me? How can you do that if you're drunk?" Her own voice was equally caustic.

"I have surprising abilities," he said, reaching for his cigarettes. "And don't even think about telling me not to smoke."

"Obviously I'd better save my breath," she said. She stared about the neat confines of her first-floor apartment. For the first time, its orderliness didn't look welcoming. It looked stark and sterile. Only the riotous color of the masks in the far corner where she worked managed to bring any life to the place.

"Nice place," Damien said, throwing himself down on the sofa and stretching his legs out in front of him.

"You hate it."

"Let's just say it's not my taste. I never did feel at home in a hospital."

"It works for me," she said, unable to keep the defensive note out of her voice.

"Terrific," he said. "I suppose I can stand it for a little while."

"Listen, don't do me any favors," she said. "I can take care of myself."

"You're going to end up with your throat cut," he said in a harsh voice. "Unless someone stops him, and nothing you've said or done has convinced me that you have the knowledge, the strength, or the sheer evil-minded brutality to outwit him."

"Do you? Have the evil-minded brutality?"

"I can give it a try." He surged to his feet, restless, like a caged tiger. "Why don't you lie down and rest? You look exhausted."

"What about you? Sleeping in the car couldn't have been the most comfortable way to spend the night."

"I slept at the motel. That should do me—I don't usually sleep more than a few hours at a time." He stalked over to the array of masks, his eyes hooded, brooding, as he surveyed them. "Don't worry," he murmured. "I won't let the bogeyman get you."

She stood there, hesitating, uncertain. On the one hand, she trusted him, truly trusted him. She could lie down and sleep, knowing she would be safe.

On the other hand, he was reaching for a mask. And he'd moved with unerring instinct to her most precious one.

She got there before him, picking up the mask of the little girl, bright orange strands of yarn framing a pale, sorrow-filled face. "I thought I might pack these away," she said, tucking the mask behind her back with what she hoped was a casual air. "Not that it would keep the Ripper away, if he was determined to get them, but at least it might slow him down."

"It might," Damien said slowly. "Which mask is that?"

"Which mask is what?" she asked, with what she hoped was an innocent expression.

"The one you have hidden behind your back."

She wondered whether she could run into the bathroom, lock the door and hide it. She didn't usually leave that mask out—as a matter of fact, she'd thought she'd put it away. But it had been there among the others; she must have forgotten to lock it away.

"Just a mask," she said, starting to back away.

She'd underestimated how tall he was, or how long his arms were. They slid around her, reaching behind to pluck the mask out of her hands, and his inadvertent embrace startled her enough to make her let go. He stepped back, and she suddenly felt chilled.

It took all her self-control not to snatch the mask out of his hands, to hide it from his too-discerning eyes. "Who is it?" he asked.

"Just a girl," she said.

"Then why are you so secretive about it?" He brushed some of the orange yarn away from the papier-mâché face, and his hand was gentle, disturbingly so. His eyes narrowed. "It's you, isn't it?"

"Don't be ridiculous." The touch of his hand was enough to make her grab for it, but he jerked it out of her reach, holding her off with his other hand.

"Of course it is," he said. "You want to explain it to me?"

"No."

"Do you want it back?"

"Yes."

"Then tell me who it is. I don't like mysteries. It's my reporter's nature. If there's a secret, I need to ferret it out."

"It's none of your damned business."

"Probably not. I still want to know who it is."

He was inexorable, and short of kicking him in the shins, there was no way she could take the mask from him without answering his questions.

She grimaced, steeling herself for his reaction. "It's me, okay?" she said in a defiant tone.

He glanced at the mask. "You're a little older than this child."

"It's supposed to be me when I was five years old."

"Was your hair really that orange?" There was a beguiling tenderness in his voice, one that unsettled her.

"It was. Please, Damien. Give it to me."

To her amazement, he did, and she clasped it against her breasts, unconsciously stroking it, comforting it.

"What happened when you were five years old?"

Damn, could he see into her soul. "What makes you think anything happened?"

"The mask."

"My mother left me in the middle of a highway, somewhere in Pennsylvania. I wasn't found for three days. My mother was never found." She clasped the mask tighter. "It's just the sort of New Age psychobabble you'd hate, Damien. I call her *The Inner Child.* I tell her she's loved, that no one will abandon her again."

She waited for his mocking response, his angry humor. But he said nothing, just looked at her out of hooded eyes. "Go lie down, Lizzie," he said finally, his voice quiet. "I'll put the mask away."

He held out his hand, and for a moment she stared at it. He had elegant hands, with long fingers and narrow palms, hands with a certain aristocratic grace. And for a brief, horrible moment she wondered what the hands of the Ripper looked like.

She put the mask back in his hand, then turned away before she could regret it. "I'm just going to check my messages," she said, heading for the machine. She paused, looking down at it, and then glanced back at Damien. Only to see him run those beautiful, deft fingers down the side of the lost child's face in a compassionate, soothing gesture.

It was the most disturbing thing she'd ever seen. She jerked her glance away to stare down at her machine. "It's not working," she said, looking at it numbly. "I remember—it didn't click in when Adamson called me this morning. I must have turned it off."

"Did you?"

His question chilled her, and she raised her eyes to meet his. "I never do."

He crossed the room, reaching in front of her to turn the machine on. The messages started playing, old messages, from Courtland, from Hickory, from one of the stores that usually sold her masks. She'd already heard them all.

"Those are old ones. No one called."

"What does your message sound like?" He turned the knob, and the whir and click of the machine presaged what she expected would be her usual slightly breathless announcement.

The voice that spoke was nothing she'd ever heard. It was neither masculine nor feminine, old nor young, innocent nor guilty. It was indisputably mad.

"Lizzie. Long Liz Stride. I'm here," the voice crooned, in a sexless, ageless rasp. "I'll be back. And you'll be found, wearing the child's mask." And the voice began to laugh.

In sudden, blind panic Lizzie grabbed the machine, ripping it free from the cords, and flung it across the room. The plastic case shattered, and loose tape began to spit across the floor like an angry snake.

Damien just looked at her. "So much for evidence," he said dryly. "Let's get the hell out of here."

She was too numb, too terrified, to react. She let him take her hand, pulling her from the apartment and slamming the door shut behind them. He bundled her into his car, climbing in after her and starting the engine. He pulled out into the midnight traffic and then turned to look at her.

"You okay?" he asked, no sympathy in his voice whatsoever.

It was just as well. She took a deep, struggling breath. "Yes," she said shakily. "I guess so. Where are we going now?"

"Away from here. We'll go to my place. It may not be spotless, but I've got better security than the CIA."

She wanted to protest. But even a motel didn't seem safe. Somehow she trusted Damien, Damien of the cool, unsympathetic voice and the dark, haunted eyes. "Yeah, it looked like it," she said, in her snottiest voice, pulling herself together by sheer force of will. "I suppose it'll have to do."

"I'm not talking about the building. But my apartment is safe—no one can get in. As long as we're holed up in there, no one can get to you."

"Except you," she pointed out with deceptive calm. "And I'm not sure if I find the idea of being trapped in that filthy apartment with you any better than the corner of Hollywood and Vine."

His smile was dark and unreassuring. "I don't have any butcher knives," he said. "And you can distract yourself by cleaning up the mess."

"Be still my heart! What woman could refuse such an offer?" she said.

"I'll keep you alive. It's a fair trade."

She looked at him as he drove with an effortless, purposeful grace. For some reason, she believed him. If anyone could keep her alive, it was this man, with his own torments, the man who had published her connection to the world, a man whose demons threatened to overwhelm him. He would keep her safe, doing a far better job than the assembled might of the Los Angeles Police Department.

"All right," she said. "Let's go."

"No more arguments? Suggestions? Complaints?"

"Just one," she said calmly. "We stop at a convenience store for cleaning supplies. If I have to die, at least I'm going to do it in a clean apartment."

The look on her face when they stepped back into his apartment was priceless, Damien thought. Like a countess stepping barefoot on a dead rat, she looked around the ramshackle rooms with a combination of horror and disdain, leavened by just a trace of determination.

She dropped the paper bag full of cleaning supplies on the sofa. "You make dinner," she said flatly, rolling up her sleeves. "I'll clean."

"I'm not hungry."

"Neither am I. You were the one who said we had to eat, to keep up our strength. So fix something," she said, pulling out a spray bottle of all-purpose cleaner and looking around the apartment with a maniacal gleam in her eyes.

"I can make three things," he said. "Scrambled eggs, scrambled eggs and Mexican scrambled eggs."

"What's the difference?" She ripped the plastic wrapper off the paper towels and began spraying.

"I put Tabasco and ketchup in the Mexican ones."

She shuddered. "Sounds ghastly," she said. "It'll be just the thing. In the meantime, why don't you make me a cup of that herbal tea I bought? Surely you can manage to boil water."

"Wouldn't you rather have a drink?"

"Save the tequila for the eggs. They'd go well together."

His face felt stiff, strange. Almost as if he'd been socked in the jaw, and not by Adamson. He put his hand up and realized what the problem was. He was grinning.

"You don't really have to keep every issue of the *Chronicle* since 1957, do you?" she continued, scooping up a pile of discarded papers from the floor beside the sagging sofa.

"I suppose not," he allowed.

She tossed them in a garbage bag, then reached for more, and he was too late to stop her. "What's this?" she said, opening up the folder that had lain haphazardly on the littered coffee table.

She dropped it on the floor, and the police photographs scattered at her feet. The sound she made was small, infinitely moving, a little noise of distress that was all the more shattering for being so quiet.

He moved quickly, pulling her into his arms, pushing her face against his shoulder so that she couldn't look down and see them. Glossy eight-by-ten full-color photographs. Of the Ripper's work, in sickening detail.

He expected her to throw up. He had, when he'd seen the latest victim. But she simply shivered in his arms, clinging so tightly that she was probably cutting off her circulation, and she kept making that quiet little sound of pain. Like a wounded fox, he thought, with her pelt of foxy red hair. He stroked it as he kept her face tight against him, feeling the shivers race through her body, and he made his own murmuring noises, senseless, soothing.

"You shouldn't have had to see that," he said finally, his voice low.

"I didn't know," she said in a numb voice.

He forced himself to push her away so that he could look down into her face. She looked pale, numb with horror, and he told himself he couldn't be moved by her. If he was, it would weaken him. And he had to find out the truth. "Why do you think they call him the Ripper?" he asked in a harsh voice. She started to glance down again, and he caught her chin, forcing her gaze away from the photographic evidence. "You don't need to look at them again," he said. "Go on in the kitchen and I'll get rid of them."

"I think," she said, in a wobbly little voice, "that I might need the bathroom."

"Straight through the bedroom." He pushed her in the right direction, watching as she broke into a stumbling run. A moment later, she'd slammed the door behind her, and he could hear her being thoroughly sick.

He wanted to go to her. He wanted to hold her head. He'd been alone with the horror, with the sickness, and he knew what it felt like, puking his guts into the toilet, still seeing the butchered bodies in his mind.

He scooped up the photographs with the detachment he'd forced himself to learn, sliding them back into the manila envelope and shoving them in a desk drawer. He went into the kitchen, brewing her tea with calm efficiency, making himself a tall drink. He'd forgotten to replenish his supply of cigarettes, and he searched through the overflowing ashtrays for a butt that was of decent length, lighting it from the glow of the gas burner on the stove, almost singeing his hair as he did it. He heard the sound of the water running, and he decided to risk seeing how she was doing. Telling himself that he wouldn't be tempted to touch her. To hold her.

She was standing in the bathroom door, surveying his tiny bedroom with a look of comical dismay on her face. "You sleep on that bed?" she asked.

"What's wrong with it? I believe it's called a double Hollywood king. I'm a tall man—I like a big bed."

"Wouldn't it work better if you didn't have twelve changes of clothes on top of it?" she said. "Sheets are also a nice option."

"I usually fall asleep on the sofa."

She shook her head. She was still pale, but she'd splashed water on her face, and her eyes were bright and determined. "You can sleep there again tonight," she said firmly. "I get the bed."

"Suit yourself," he said, leaning against the door frame. "You can throw the clothes out if you want."

She stared at him, scandalized. "These are good clothes," she said. "Italian suits."

"British, actually. And I don't wear suits anymore." He turned, planning to leave her to her ridiculous housewifely urges, when her voice forestalled him.

"Damien," she said quietly, "what happened to you?"

Her soft words stabbed him as lethally as the Ripper's blade. He made one attempt at fighting. "I don't know what you mean."

"It's not just the Ripper. It's been longer than that, even I can tell that much. What happened to you?"

"Persistent, aren't you?" He turned back and looked at her coolly. "Nothing that astonishing. I watched a woman die."

"Who?"

"No one I knew. I believe her name was Betty Brinston, though she was going by the name Ashanti Mizrak."

"How did she die?"

He wanted to scream at her. He wanted to put his hands over his ears to drown out her quiet words, to drown out the thoughts, the memories, the guilt, that had been plaguing him for too damned long. But he couldn't. He'd finally made the mistake of getting close to someone he couldn't turn off, couldn't shut out. All he could do was answer her simple question.

"She set herself on fire," he said. "I don't even remember what the hell she was protesting. Some military involvement, maybe, or a new nuclear facility. Hell, she might even have been protesting about saving the spotted owls. It doesn't really matter. She was a nut case, certifiable. It all came out in the inquest."

"Did you know her?"

"No," he said. "I stood there, with a camera in my hand, and I watched her die. And I didn't do a damned thing to stop her." He turned away so that she wouldn't see his face. "Your tea's ready."

He took the time to pour the tequila into a glass, but he didn't bother with ice, with water, with salt or lime. He tipped it down his throat, letting it burn its way into his stomach, waiting for the numbness to begin. He drained it, then reached for the bottle to pour himself some more, determined to get blindly, stupidly drunk, to shut out the voices.

Her hand reached out and covered his, stopping him. She had strong hands, with long, beautiful fingers, short nails. The hands of a craftsperson. The hands of an artist.

"You can't drink away your demons," she said gently.

"How the hell do you know?" His voice was savage. "I can damned well try."

"It doesn't work," she said. "Demons are too strong." And she released his hand, picking up her mug of tea and walking slowly back into the living room.

He watched her go. His eyes skimmed the straight, elegant line of her back, the set of her shoulders, the graceful carriage of her head. And he wondered if her demons came anywhere near his own. Or whether it was something as simple as having been abandoned by a mother and having bad taste in men.

Bad taste that extended to him. He might even go and help her clear off that oversize bed in his room. Because he wasn't going to sleep on his sagging sofa. They were going to sleep together on that bed, either on clean sheets or on the mattress amid the pile of discarded clothes, he didn't care which. She was right—he couldn't silence his demons with tequila. But he could damned well try with her.

CHAPTER EIGHT

"You lied to me," Lizzie said, watching him.

There was instant wariness in his dark eyes. He stood at the kitchen counter, shoveling the scrambled eggs into his mouth with a total disregard for taste or texture, following them with burned toast. He'd scraped the mold off one corner, but Lizzie had still refused the offering.

"How did I do that?"

"You can't even cook eggs."

He was managing a little better than that sour smile she'd first seen. It almost reached his bleak eyes this time, and she was determined that, sooner or later, she would make him laugh. "They're edible," he said.

"Just barely. Don't you have anything else here?"

"Not that I know of. Eggs do me fine. Morning, noon and night."

She'd seen the three cartons in the refrigerator. "And you smoke, too. You must have a cholesterol level of catastrophic proportions," she said.

"I don't give a damn."

"If you don't care what you eat, you might as well eat something good for you," she countered stubbornly. She'd given up on her own meal long ago and was busy trying to make a dent in what was arguably the filthiest room in the place.

"Sure thing," he drawled. "We'll head out for the health food store in the BMW. Just as soon as I finish my last bottle of Evian . . ."

"Cut it out."

"You just don't get it, do you?" he said. "I don't care. I don't care whether I drop dead from a stroke in five years. I don't care whether I get lung cancer. I don't care about a damn thing. Except finding the Ripper."

She watched him in silence. He was so cool, so tough, so remote. He would break her heart if she let him. "You're forgetting one thing," she said. "You care about saving my life."

"Don't flatter yourself," he said, dumping his plate in the sink. It was still half full of congealed eggs. "I just don't want him to kill anymore. It wouldn't matter to me if you were the queen of the hookers or some bag lady. I don't want to see another woman die."

It felt like a blow to the stomach, and she searched quickly for something distracting to say, to keep him from seeing her reaction. "What do you mean, see? You haven't watched those women die."

He ignored her comment. "What's wrong with you?"

"Nothing."

He pushed himself away from the counter, coming closer to her in the tiny little kitchen area. She'd washed all the dishes and scrubbed the countertops, and she was busy concentrating on the layers of grease that coated the white enamel stovetop when he took the rag out of her hand and turned her around to meet his searching gaze.

"Come on, Lizzie," he said, his voice unnervingly gentle. "I've spilled my deep dark secrets. It's time for some of yours."

"You have more secrets than you've been telling me," she said. He was holding her wrist, and his fingers were long and strong, imprisoning and yet not the slightest bit hurtful.

"We all have secrets. Time for one of yours."

She bit her lip. There was absolutely no reason why she should tell him. After all, he was a reporter—it was his job to find out things. If he hadn't uncovered that particularly dark time in her life, then there was no reason why he should know. No one else did, with the single exception of Courtland.

But Damien wasn't about to take no for an answer. "Come on, Lizzie," he said, putting his other hand under her chin, lifting her face to meet his dark gaze. "Tell me."

And she knew she was going to. "You didn't do your research very well," she said in a harsh voice.

"That surprises me," he said. "I'm usually very thorough."

"Not this time. You failed to check my police record. Not in California. In Michigan. Where I grew up."

His face was cool, expressionless. "Sounds ominous. Why don't you tell me about it? What were you, a juvenile delinquent? A gun moll?"

"Queen of the hookers."

He didn't even blink. "You want to explain that?"

"Not particularly. I learned long ago that people wouldn't believe me."

"You forget, I used to be a reporter. I've spent a lot of time listening to unbelievable stories. So what did you do, turn tricks in high school to pay for your red Corvette?"

She wanted to hit him. On the one hand, his cool, dispassionate tone took all the melodrama out of it. On the other, she wouldn't have minded some sympathy. "I didn't have a Corvette," she snapped. "As a matter of fact, I didn't even have a family. My mother abandoned me when I was five years old, remember? And none of my foster parents seemed interested in anything more than the monthly sum I brought in."

"Tough life," he said, in that same detached voice. "So you became a hooker in response to your deprived childhood?"

"No!" she snapped. "I made the major mistake of thinking I was in love. You've already noticed I have lousy taste in men. That's nothing compared with Billy Order and Mark Clayton."

"Two of them?" He raised an eyebrow. "How adventurous of you."

"I thought Billy was my best friend, my buddy," she said hotly. "And I thought Mark loved me. I didn't realize he was paying Billy every time we slept together. Both for the use of Billy's house, and for the use of me."

He reacted with no more than cool curiosity. "How'd you manage to get busted?"

His matter-of-fact attitude made it easier to tell him. "Billy decided to branch out. He was working the same deal with a couple of other girls, girls who knew the score and were smart enough to demand their share. One of them assumed I knew what was going on. When I confronted Billy and Mark, they denied it, and when I went to the police, they arrested me." The shame of that day still burned in her soul. She'd been seventeen, an honor student—and in love. In twenty-four hours she was a criminal, her foster parents had kicked her out, and the school had suspended her.

"Tough," he said again, his voice oddly gentle. His hand still cupped her chin, the long fingers lightly caressing against her jaw. "But you're forgetting one thing."

"What's that?" She didn't like the feel of his skin against her flesh. Because she liked it too much.

"They dropped the charges. And your good buddy Billy ended up getting busted for dealing less than a year later, and he did some hard time."

She jerked away from him in shock. "You did know!" she cried accusingly. "Why did you make me tell you?"

His smile was cool, self-deprecating. "Confession's good for the soul. Besides, your take on it's a hell of a lot different from the facts. The facts are, you were picked up on suspicion of soliciting, and within twenty-four hours the charges were dropped. You were a minor, and there isn't even a record of anything happening."

"If there's no record, how did you know?"

"I find out what I need to," he said. "So if things were different, you could simply forget that unpleasant time in your life, chalk it up to bad experience and lousy taste in men, and forget about it."

"What do you mean, if things were different?"

"You were once busted for soliciting. If I know it, then the Ripper knows it. And the Ripper preys on hookers. Not good girls. Not housewives. Hookers."

"Damn," she said, closing her eyes.

"Damn, indeed." His voice was cool, dispassionate. "Why don't you go in and lie down? You look exhausted. I can finish up in here."

"I know from looking around me that you're cleaning abilities are even worse than your cooking," she said faintly.

"True enough. But the place has survived months of neglect. I swear, there are no rats, even if it looks as if the place harbors a nest of them. Go to bed, Lizzie. In the morning, everything will look better."

"Not in *this* apartment," she said darkly. He'd released her hand, she noted with distant regret. She wanted him to hold her hand. For some inexplicable reason, she wanted him to do far more than that. She wanted him to make the night go away.

But he'd turned away from her, staring out into the darkness, tension riveting every line of his tall, wiry body, and she knew there was no comfort there. She had no choice but to believe him—she meant nothing to him, other than a life to be saved, if possible. A body to be used to lure the Ripper into the open. He probably wasn't aware of her as a woman at all.

Scratch that. He'd kissed her, hadn't he? Kissed her quite thoroughly, until they were both shaking. He knew she was a woman, all right. Even though he was doing his best to warn her away.

And she was seven times a fool not to listen to those warnings. Not to remember her ridiculous habit of falling for the worst of all possible men. First Mark, with his blond arrogance and his football-star charisma. Then Freddy, an actor with enough charm to fool even the wariest female, and enough self-absorption to make her regret her weakness. Freddy had been three years ago, and since then she'd tried very hard not to let herself weaken. She'd been on the verge of it with James, but she'd pulled back in time, before she'd had the chance to get physically involved. He'd moved out when he realized she didn't want to sleep with him, and she'd been relieved to see him go.

She preferred it that way. Sex was overrated, though she certainly expected it could be better than her limited experience had taught her. But all in all, she was just as glad she didn't know. Life was simpler if she did without it, if she put her energies, her frustrations, her desires, into her masks.

So why was she standing in the kitchen of this derelict apartment, staring at the harsh, unrelenting line of a man's back, the back of a man so obsessed and withdrawn that she was a fool to trust him? A fool not to consider that he might be the very man the police were looking for?

He turned to her then, his eyes distant. "What are you looking at?" And then realization darkened his face, and he smiled that cool, mocking travesty of a smile. "You finally put two and two together."

She wouldn't panic. She could feel the icy fear start in the pit of her stomach, coiling upward, stretching icy fingers to wrap around her heart. If she gave in to it, there would be nothing. "What do you mean?" she asked, stiffening her spine, hoping he wouldn't notice the faint tremor in her voice.

But Damien was a man who noticed everything. "You finally considered—really considered—whether I might be the Venice Ripper. After all, I have the knowledge. I know more about the killings than even the police seem to. I have the medical background—I was premed at Stanford. I have no alibi—I live alone. And my life-style and actions are very suspicious. I certainly wouldn't seem to be the model of mental and emotional stability, now would I? Add to that, I have a history of collecting your masks, and what do you end up with?''

She wet her lips, refusing to step away from him, much as her terrified heart pounded at her to do so. "I don't know," she said. "You tell me."

"A prime suspect. Alone in his apartment with someone who is probably the Ripper's most favored victim. And no one knows we're here."

"Adamson . . ."

"Although he's the best cop in town, Adamson couldn't find his own nose in the dark," Damien said briefly. "If I am the Ripper, I've managed to cover my tracks already. There has to be a terrific amount of blood involved, and yet no one's been seen in the area looking like a butcher."

"Don't," she said weakly.

He moved closer to her, so close that his body brushed against hers, radiating warmth, tension, danger. "Think about it, Lizzie. You've put yourself in my hands," he said, his voice low and insinuating. "And it's taken you until this very moment to consider how dangerous that might be."

Somehow she knew that if she gave in to her very rational fear there would be no hope for her. And if she gave in to her irrational trust, she would be safe. "Why are you doing this? Why are you trying to scare me?"

He reached out and touched her, cupping her face, his fingers sliding through her thick hair. "You can't trust anyone," he said. "Not the cops, not me, certainly not your own judgment. If you're going to stay alive, you have to be smart enough to suspect everyone."

"That's no way to live," she whispered, staring up at him. At his mouth, which was dangerously, enticingly close to hers. She wanted to feel that mouth once more.

She wanted to silence the frightening words he was saying.

"It's the *only* way to live," he replied. "The only way you're going to survive. Otherwise, even I can't save you."

He was going to kiss her. She knew it; she could read it in his bleak eyes, could see the dark longing that matched her own. He was going to kiss her, and the years would dissolve, and it would be just the two of them, as it was meant to be. Her heart stopped, then started again with a mad thudding, and she held her breath, waiting, watching, as his mouth drew closer, closer. . . .

And then he pulled away, and she could see the effort it cost him. "Go to bed, Lizzie," he said. "I won't let the bad guys get you. Tonight."

She left him then, before she made an even greater fool of herself than she had already. When she looked at him, her mind flew out the window. He frightened her as no man had ever managed to frighten her before. He drew her in the same way. She didn't know what she would discover at those long, elegant hands. Transcendence? Or death?

But tonight wasn't the time to find out, particularly since he'd already dismissed her so abruptly. Tonight was the night to hide away in that tiny bedroom, burrow down under the covers and try not to think about the creature that roamed the night. Using her masks.

And try not to think about those photographs. Though she suspected they would haunt her for the rest of her life.

Damien sat alone in his unnaturally neat living room, staring at the TV. He'd barely moved for the past hour.

He had no cigarettes, but not even for the most desperate nicotine craving would he leave Lizzie alone and unprotected in his apartment. Even though he couldn't be completely certain she didn't need to be protected from him.

He wouldn't let himself sleep. He didn't know what happened when he slept. All he knew was that the memory came, the dream, of things that had yet to happen. And he could think of only one logical reason.

He wasn't psychic. In general, he had nothing but a benign contempt for both the charlatans themselves and the self-deluded fools who professed to believe in such things. There was always a reasonable explanation for the most inexplicable occurrences.

But his particular reasonable explanation scared the hell out of him. The only way he could know the brutal, foul details of the murders was if he was there, committing them.

In his dreams he could smell the blood, the harsh, metallic scent of it. Feel the warmth as it drained from the mutilated bodies. He could look down at the grisly evidence of the Ripper's work and not flinch.

In daylight it took all his concentration not to gag. But still, at the bottom of it all, was the troubling knowledge that whenever Adamson gave him new information about one of the crimes, it was always something he already knew.

He wouldn't sleep. If he slept, there was no telling what he might do. But his entire body vibrated with awareness of the woman asleep in his bed.

He'd heard her running the shower, and he'd wondered what she'd found to put on. Something of his, no doubt.

Was she wearing one of his T-shirts? How far down her endless legs would it reach? Had she put his discarded clothes away, found sheets for the bed? Was she lying there right now, curled up on the huge mattress, her thick red hair spread out over one of his pillows? Did she sleep on her stomach or her back? Did she sleep soundly?

He turned off the television, suddenly feeling unbearably restless. He wouldn't sleep tonight; he was too edgy to feel so much as tempted. He'd had enough coffee, and his craving for cigarettes simply added to his edge. He wouldn't sleep, and therefore he wouldn't endanger her. That didn't mean he couldn't give in to temptation and watch her.

The bedroom was dark as he slowly opened the door, the only light coming from the automatic night light in the bathroom. He'd bought that soon after the first Ripper killing. He'd grown to hate the darkness.

He could see her in the middle of the bed, quite clearly. There was no sign of his clothes, and she'd made up the bed. She lay on the left side, slender, long bare legs stretched out. Wearing an old white oxford shirt of his, the tails reaching almost to her knees.

He always slept on the right side. Despite having the full bed, he unconsciously left room for someone beside him. She'd done the same.

He leaned against the door jamb, watching her. His head ached, his eyes burned, but still he didn't move. Would it hurt so much if he lay down next to her? She'd left plenty of room—he wouldn't be touching her. He hadn't slept in his bed for weeks now, and suddenly he wanted to, needed to. Needed to sleep next to her, a living, breathing person. To hear her heartbeat, feel her body heat. To know her.

He was already barefoot. He moved across the room silently, skirting the huge bed. She lay there, her breathing deep and heavy, unaware that he was watching her—lusting after her, damn it. She would be no match for the Ripper if he came to call.

He wasn't going to. Damien was going to keep her safe. Safe from death, even if he was the killer. As long as he didn't sleep himself.

He lowered himself onto the bed beside her, gingerly, watching her closely, but she didn't stir. A man could come up behind her and slit her throat before she so much as noticed, he thought in despair. How in God's name was he ever going to save her life?

For now, for tonight, he wasn't going to worry about it. He was simply going to lie there and watch her, breathing in the faint trace of soap and toothpaste that clung to her, mixed with other, subtler scents that slid behind his defenses. He was going to lie there, more aroused than he could remember ever being, and keep her safe. Everything about her was so achingly familiar, and yet he knew he'd never lain with her before. Longed for her, kissed her. But never slept with her.

He closed his eyes, just for a brief moment, just so that he could concentrate on his other senses. The weight of her body in the bed next to him. The quiet sound of her breathing. He'd gotten so that he didn't need more than a couple of hours sleep a night, and he'd already had his allotment at the motel today. He had no need of sleep. He would stay awake, alert. He would open his eyes in just one more moment. He wouldn't sleep.

Lizzie opened her eyes cautiously, peering at him from beneath thick lashes. J. R. Damien snored.

It was a revelation. She wouldn't have thought he was capable of such a human bodily function. It wasn't a loud snore—more a muffled snort as he sank deeper into sleep. She raised herself up on one elbow, pushing her still-wet hair away from her face, to watch him.

She'd woken up the moment he'd appeared in the doorway, his tall body casting a shadow across hers. In the first moments of sleep-dazed surprise, she'd felt no fear at all. When her defenses were down, when she was at her most vulnerable, half-asleep and almost naked in this man's bed, she trusted him implicitly.

It had been a relief and a wonder. No matter how he tried to frighten her, even if it was for her own good, he wouldn't succeed. She trusted him. It was that simple.

Now she stared at him in the darkness, wondering if he slept soundly. Wondering if he would wake up if she touched him. She longed to reach out and caress his silky black hair, to soothe the lines from his high forehead, to trace the sharp contour of mouth and lip.

She couldn't, of course. What if he awoke and caught her?

Neither could she lie in the bed, so close to him, and not move closer. People moved in their sleep; they snuggled up to whatever was closest. Surely she could manage to be that convincing an actress. This was the first time she'd been in bed with a man in over three years, the first time she'd really wanted to be in bed with a man. She was hardly going to spend the night with all that space between them.

She sighed, loudly, letting her eyes drift closed as she snuggled down deeper into the bed. He didn't move, so deep in sleep that the National Guard could have marched through the bedroom without waking him.

Go for it, she ordered herself, rolling across the narrow space that separated them, making sleepy, innocent little noises until she ended up next to the hard, muscular heat of his body. He made a sound himself, something rather like a *humph,* as she settled against him. And then his arms came around her, pulling her body up against his, tucking her head beneath his shoulder, as he slept on, oblivious.

For a moment, she was stiff with tension. And then, slowly, deliberately, she forced her body to relax. This was what she'd wanted, what she needed. Not sex. Not romance. Just a strong male body, tight against hers. To help her make it through the darkness. He'd done in his sleep what she'd done in subterfuge, holding her close. He would have no reason to blame her if he woke up and found their bodies entwined. Chances were, she would wake before he did, and he would never realize what he'd done.

She realized with sudden shock that he was aroused. She felt color suffuse her face in the darkness, felt the sudden racing of her heart, the burning ache in the pit of her stomach as she responded.

It was a simple biological function, she reminded herself. The man was asleep, deeply asleep, with a female body wrapped around him. Of course he was aroused. It meant absolutely nothing. Any female body would have done the same. He wasn't even aware of her....

"Relax, Lizzie." His voice was cool, soothing, in the darkness, and it shocked her.

For a moment she dissolved into embarrassed silence. She tried to pull away from him, but his relaxed muscles grew suddenly tense as he held her firmly against him, and she could feel the pounding of his own heart, the throbbing of his pulse, against her. "Go back to sleep," he said, his own voice sleepy.

He was too strong, too implacable, and she really had no desire to leave the dangerous heat of his body. She took a deep, shaky breath, forcing her muscles to relax.

"That's right, Lizzie," he murmured approvingly. "No one will hurt you. Go back to sleep."

She wanted to protest. She wanted to argue. But even more, she wanted to fall asleep in his arms. And in the end she gave in. Knowing she would be safe. From everyone but J. R. Damien.

CHAPTER NINE

The dreams came. The vision, thick with blood and terror, just as he'd known it would. He was there, standing over the mutilated remains of the girl, staring down at her, and he could smell the blood. Her ears had been cut away, and the blood matted her thick black hair. Her eyes were wide open, staring up at him from the savaged ruins of her body, and they were filled with horror and accusation. Her mouth was open in a bloody scream that no one ever heard, but she called his name, called out his guilt, through the decades, howling in pain and fury, until he had to hold his ears to drown out her cries, until he had to scream himself, the sound ripped from his throat, and his hands were covered with her blood. She was dead, lying there in a welter of carnage, and he was responsible.

The sound of his scream woke her, ripping her from sleep in sudden terror. Damien had scrambled off the bed, and he was sitting on the floor, his back against the wall, his eyes wide open but faraway, focused on something too terrible to contemplate. His breath was coming in short, rapid pants, and he looked as if he'd stared into the depths of hell, only to see his own face reflected back.

Lizzie didn't hesitate. She threw herself off the bed, kneeling in front of him, taking his beautiful, slack, ice-cold hands in hers. "Wake up, Damien," she said urgently, even though he was clearly awake. She dropped his hands, reached up for his shoulders and shook them, hard, so that his head snapped back and banged against the wall and his eyes suddenly sharpened and focused on her.

"You," he said, in a harsh, strangled voice. And then he hauled her into his arms, between his legs, pressing her up against him, and buried his face in her hair. He was shaking so hard that the chill reached Lizzie's body, as well, and she pushed closer to him, cradled between his thighs, her arms around his head, holding him protectively as he trembled. Feeling his hot breath against her skin, the terror that spiked through him, terror that slowly, slowly abated.

"What did you dream?" she asked, when his shaking had finally quieted.

He lifted his head to look at her, and in the darkness his eyes were bleak. "No dream," he said. He took his hands away from her, and he stared down at them in surprise.

Lizzie made no effort to move away from him. "Then what?" she demanded. "A vision? A nightmare?"

"A memory," he said, rubbing his hands along his jean-covered thighs, as if he wanted to wash away traces of something. "I saw the Ripper's latest victim," he said quietly. "Lying in an alleyway, behind a strip joint."

"The latest victim was found in West Covina," Lizzie said.

Damien shook his head. "There's another one. Closer. Much closer." He stared down at his hands again and shuddered.

Lizzie could stand it no more. She put her hands on his face, staring at him. "What are you trying to say?" she demanded. "What are you afraid of? How could you remember something that hasn't even happened?"

"It's happened," he said. "Oh, God, it's already happened." He tried to rise, to push her away, but she wouldn't let him.

"What's happened?" she said. "Damien, tell me."

For a moment he hesitated, and she held her breath, waiting. And then he shook his head. "I should tell you to leave," he said obscurely. "I should send you away, out of here, away from me. Before I—"

"Before you what?" she demanded when he abruptly stopped speaking. She was kneeling between his legs, her hands on his face, pleading, vulnerable.

He stared at her, and then something seemed to sweep across his bleak face. Wariness, acceptance. "Before you get hurt," he said, in a calmer voice, and she knew that wasn't what he'd been about to say at all. "I don't give a damn what Adamson says, you need to get out of town. Out of this state, out of the country. In the morning I'm driving you out to LAX and putting you on the first plane away from here."

"I won't go," she said, dropping her hands in her lap.

"Don't be a fool, Lizzie. I don't have anything to spend my money on, and there can't be a much better investment than saving a life. You can call it an advance on some new masks. I don't really give a damn. I just want you away from here. Away from Los Angeles. Away from ... the Ripper."

"I thought you were going to stay away from me," she said quietly. "Why should you be a threat to me?"

"Because I'll sacrifice anyone or anything to get the Ripper," he said.

She knew he was lying. "Damien," she said. "Damien, you would never sacrifice me."

For a moment, neither of them moved. And then he reached up to touch her, his hands cupping her shoulders, drawing her down, bringing her mouth to his. He kissed her slowly, gently, his mouth soft and damp and questing against her lips. He nibbled at her, tasting her. It was a kiss of such startling sweetness that she felt tears spring to her eyes, as a gnawing, yearning warmth started in the pit of her stomach and grew, spiraling outward, downward, filling her with such heat and longing that she began to tremble herself, and she wanted to move closer, to sink against him, into him, to press against him and dissolve.

His hands tightened on her shoulders, moving her back slightly, and she looked at him through emotion-shrouded eyes. "Don't trust me," he said in a harsh voice. And then he kissed her again, harder this time, without the sweetness, the tenderness, but with a fullness of passion that left her taut and aching. He murmured something against her mouth, and she opened her lips, letting his tongue inside, as her eyes fluttered closed. His hands moved down from her shoulders to cover her breasts through the flimsy barrier of his shirt, and her nipples hardened against him in the dark, hot room. And then his hands moved lower, under the hem of the shirt, sliding up her bare torso until he touched her breasts, the skin hot and tender, her nipples thrusting against him, and she made a quiet little cry of longing, arching closer. He pulled her nearer, over him, so that she was straddling his lap, her arms around his neck as she kissed him back, no longer thinking about anything but the demand of his mouth against hers, the strength of his body between her legs, the heat and hardness of him against the juncture of her thighs, the feel of his callused hands against her swollen breasts.

His denim shirt was soft and worn beneath her hands. She yanked it open unsnapping the snaps, and touched his chest, letting her hands revel in his smooth, sleek skin. She could feel the furious pace of his heart beneath her touch, feel it match the racing pulse of her own, and she knew he'd managed to unbutton the shirt she wore so that when she leaned against him her breasts were against the muscled hardness of his chest, her heart was against him, just as her mouth knew his, and she felt his hands reach down to the zipper of his jeans, and she started to shift, to give him room, when he stopped, reaching out and clutching her arms, grasping them, as he pulled his mouth away from hers. And then he put her away from him, moving her gently off his lap as he climbed to his feet and walked from the room, leaving her kneeling on the carpet, cold, shaking, awash with conflicting emotions, one of which, she knew, was the never-before-experienced sensation of sexual frustration.

She rebuttoned the shirt with shaking hands, then reached for her jeans and pulled them on. Part of her wanted to crawl back into the bed and pull the covers over her head, rather than face him. But she was too strung out, too tense, too angry, to pretend nothing had happened and simply go back to sleep.

He was standing in the darkened living room, looking out over the city through the cracked picture window. He hadn't bothered to resnap the shirt she'd almost torn off him, and she could see him quite clearly, tall and lean and impossibly beautiful. He didn't turn when she walked up to him, but his voice was low and cool. "You don't want this, Lizzie," he said.

"Don't tell me what I do or don't want," she shot back, furious. "Who are you to tell me what I need? I didn't start this...."

"No," he said, staring out into the darkness, keeping his face averted. "But I finished it. Damn it, woman, you have no more sense of self-preservation than a week-old kitten." He turned to face her, and his eyes glittered in the darkness. "How long has it been since you've slept with a man? How long?"

She considered lying, but she decided he already knew the truth. "Why bother to ask, when you know the answer? Almost three years. What has that got to do with anything? Maybe I'm hard to please."

"It has a great deal to do with things. Maybe you're a fool when it comes to men. You're not someone who jumps into bed with the first man she finds attractive. You keep your distance, which is even more proof that it isn't desire that's making you want me, it's panic."

They said counting to ten was an effective way to control one's temper. That, or reciting the books of the Bible. Lizzie didn't know the books of the Bible, and counting to a thousand wouldn't calm her down now.

"I never thought panic was an aphrodisiac," she said tartly.

His smile was devastating, she thought, staring at him. He reached for her, then let his hand drop before she could go to him. "Where you and I are concerned, Lizzie, everything is an aphrodisiac," he said wryly. "I want you to go back to bed."

"Why?"

"Because if you don't, I might take you there. And that would be a mistake for both of us."

"Why?" she asked again.

"Because I'm not in the market for a roll in the hay, a two-night stand, a relationship, or true love. I don't need anyone. I don't have the time or the energy for anyone other than myself right now. I don't want you, Lizzie. And I don't want to hurt you."

I don't want you, Lizzie. He thought he could say that to her and still not hurt her? She stared at him stonily. "I'm glad you made that clear," she said evenly.

"And you don't really want me. You want safety, you want comfort, and you may have a very normal longing for sex, but it has absolutely nothing to do with me. I'm just an available male, trying to protect you, and you're imagining that I might fill those other needs. I can't. I never will. Go back to bed, Lizzie. Before I take what you're offering and to hell with better judgment."

"I'm not offering you a damned thing," she shot back, furious and embarrassed.

"Aren't you?" Before she realized what he intended, he'd pulled her into his arms again, threaded one hand through her thick red hair and tilted her head back beneath his. He set his mouth on hers, and his kiss was brief, thorough and totally sexual. And when he lifted his head, only the rapidity of his breathing betrayed his own reaction. "You see?" he said, calmly enough. "I could have you on your back in a matter of moments. Run away from me, Lizzie. Tomorrow I'll put you on a plane, and you won't ever have to see me again."

"Don't planes fly all night long?"

He still had his arms around her. The tension sizzled between them like a charge of electricity, and yet his grip didn't loosen. "Why are you baiting me, Lizzie?" he asked finally.

"Because I want to know what you're hiding from me," she said. "I want to know what you were about to say, back in the bedroom. I want to know what you think you're going to do to me, that you have to send me across the country to keep me safe. You're not sending me away from the Ripper. You're sending me away from you."

He didn't move for a long moment, and then he released her, turning away, staring out the window once more. "You know, you're too damned smart for your own good," he said.

"I've asked you before, and I'll ask you again, Damien. What are you afraid of?"

The telephone rang, the sound sharp and shrill in the darkness. He started, making a step toward it, but she reached out and caught his arm. "Let the answering machine get it," she said. "Tell me what you're afraid of. Are you afraid you might care about me?" It was a bold, embarrassing question, but she was determined to force an answer from him.

She could feel the strength in his arm beneath her hand. And then he pulled free. "No," he said. "I'm afraid I might kill you." And he picked up the telephone, just as the answering machine clicked on.

Both voices came from the machine, amplified—Adamson's and Damien's. "We've got another one, Damien." His voice was weary. "I'm trying to find Lizzie."

"She's here."

There was a momentary silence on the other end. "I thought she might be. Can I talk to her?"

"I'll give her your message. She's asleep right now, and I don't want to wake her." He lied easily enough, not even glancing at Lizzie to see whether she objected or not.

"No wonder. She's probably worn out. We'll have to have her identify the mask. She knows the drill—God knows she's used to it by now."

"Where was the body found this time?"

"You know I can't tell you that, Damien. Why bother to ask? Just another hooker, her body ripped apart by some monster."

"You can tell me whether he's come back to Venice or not," he said. "Whether she was found on the beach, or in some back alley."

"Back alley," Adamson said, his voice sharpening. "How did you know?"

"Most of them have been found in back alleyways."

"True enough. It's on the police scanner. I don't imagine it'll do me any good to try to keep it quiet. She was found out behind the Greasy Cat. You know, the strip joint over by the freeway."

"I know," Damien said in a hollow voice.

"I sort of hate to make her ID it, but I've got to. It's a real mess this time. Soaked with blood."

"Aren't they all?" Damien said, refusing to meet her troubled gaze.

"This is worse than usual. He cut off her ears."

Damien closed his eyes, feeling the blood drain from his face. "In the morning," he said hoarsely, and slammed down the telephone.

And then he began to shake.

All thought of the murdered girl fled Lizzie's mind. Whoever she was, she was dead, butchered, beyond pain and beyond anyone's help. The man in front of her was tormented by demons he refused to name.

She wanted to go to him, to put her arms around him and draw his head down on her breast. She was wise enough not to move. "What is it?" she asked.

He roused himself. "You heard Adamson. Another murder."

"It's more than that. You look as if you'd seen a ghost."

He shook his head. "Not a ghost," he said, in a flat, dead voice. "Just the murder."

"Damien . . ."

He held up his hand. "Don't come any closer, Lizzie. You have no sense of self-preservation at all, but this time, at least, do as I say. I don't . . . trust myself."

She sucked in her breath in shock. "What do you mean?"

"You know what my name is, Lizzie?" he asked, out of the blue. "J. R. Damien. John Ripley Damien. I was called Jack when I was a little boy."

She waited for the panic to fill her, but none came. "Damien," she said gently, "are you trying to tell me you really think you're the Ripper?"

"I don't know," he said angrily. "I saw her. I've seen them all. Smelled the stench of death, seen the ripped-apart bodies. And my hands have been covered with blood."

"There's a logical enough explanation," she said. "You're psychic. You're having precognitions, visions."

"Like Lees?" he said bitterly.

"Who's Lees?"

"Robert Lees. Psychic to Queen Victoria. An odd, twitching sort of fellow. He had visions of the original murders. He was one of the original suspects. One of a hundred." He made an abrupt, dismissive gesture with his hand. "I'm thirty-seven years old, Lizzie, and I've never had a vision in my life. Not only do I not possess psychic abilities, I don't believe in them."

"Then how do you see the crimes?"

"There's only one logical explanation. That I was there. That I committed them. Even if I have no conscious memory of doing them."

"Damien," she said, taking a tentative step toward him. "You were asleep beside me tonight. You haven't left my side since late this afternoon."

"You were asleep when I came into the bedroom," he countered roughly. "What makes you think you hadn't slept for a couple of hours, long enough for me to commit the murder and get back to the apartment?"

"I wasn't asleep that long."

"The Ripper can accomplish his work in lightning-fast time. I could have done it in less than an hour, including the drive and cleaning up afterward."

She crossed the room then, taking his hands in hers. "Don't you think there'd be a trace of blood? Beneath your fingernails, for instance?" His hands were deft, beautiful and spotless, and they jerked beneath her touch.

"Maybe I wore surgical gloves."

For a moment his flat words penetrated her self-assurance, and she felt a frisson of horror fill her. And then she shook it off. "You aren't the Ripper," she said.

"Then who the hell am I? And how do I know what I know?"

She stared at him in mute frustration. "I can't answer that," she said. "But I know someone who can."

"Lizzie . . ."

"Have you talked to anyone? Told anyone what you suspect?"

"I'm not particularly interested in landing in a mental hospital or in jail," he said with a trace of his usual self-possession. "Unless I'm sure. And if I were, I think I'd be better off wrapping my Austin-Healey around a tree."

"Do you know about the next murder? Anything that you could warn the police about?"

"I told you, I'm not Robert Lees! I know what's happening *when* it happens. I'm there, Lizzie."

"In spirit, perhaps. I don't believe you're there in body," she said.

"I've already told you, you're too innocent."

"There's one sure way to find out," she said, moving away from him. "I'll call Courtland."

"You won't call anyone."

"She's got an amazing gift. She's the real thing, Damien, even if you won't believe it. If she were the kind of charlatan you think they all are, then she'd be willing to make money off her talents, rather than struggling to get by as a waitress at the Pink Pelican. She can hypnotize you, find out what you've got hidden so deep inside...."

"No."

"Cast the runes for you, do a tarot reading."

"Lizzie, that's just a bunch of crap. It's worthless."

"It's worth a try." She reached for the telephone, and he came up behind her, grabbing it out of her hand. He was very strong, and he hurt her, just a little bit.

"The Ripper comes up behind his victims," he said, in a cool, almost meditative voice. "Both the Venice Ripper and the London one."

Lizzie froze, waiting for panic. None came. She could feel his heat, the muscled hardness of his body, his tension. "Damien," she said evenly, "she might be able to give you the answers. You're a fool not to try."

For a moment, he didn't move. And then he released her, moving away, and she was suddenly unbearably cold. "Do what you want," he said wearily. "Anything's worth a shot, no matter how farfetched. I'm going to get drunk."

She picked up the telephone before he could change his mind and try to stop her again. She felt no fear at all. Damien wasn't the Venice Ripper, despite his terrible visions and memories. Damien wasn't a violent man, he was a man possessed, tormented by dreams and memories that weren't his doing.

Courtland would sort them out. Courtland would come up with the answers, the possibility of a happy ending. The alternative was unacceptable. If Courtland couldn't find reassurance, then, despite Lizzie's certainty, Damien might be right after all. And if that was true, having Courtland delve into other dimensions could sign both their death warrants.

CHAPTER TEN

"So this is where Damien lives?" Courtland said when she walked into the apartment two hours later, just before dawn. She looked around her with bright curiosity. "It doesn't look like that sort of place where an upscale reporter would reside."

"I'm not upscale," Damien said from the kitchen doorway, his voice low and dour. "Did you come alone?"

Lizzie stiffened, though she'd been prepared for Damien to be his most unsociable. "Courtland, this is J. R. Damien. Damien, this is Courtland Massey."

Courtland looked up at Damien with an appraising gleam in her bright blue eyes, one that was frankly sexual, and Lizzie knew a sudden moment of misgiving. Courtland was as traditionally beautiful—blond-haired, blue-eyed beautiful—as an aspiring actress should be. Lizzie had never seen her set her sights on a man and fail to get him. Now Courtland's gaze sharpened as she looked at Damien, and her beautiful mouth curved in a faintly challenging smile. "So this is the patient. You don't appear to be looking forward to this, Damien."

"I'm not. I don't believe in it."

Courtland moved closer, and Lizzie could smell the seductive, musky fragrance of her perfume. She'd sprayed it on more liberally than usual, a sure sign of danger. "Most people say they don't," she murmured.

"But deep in their souls they're just as gullible as anyone."

"Trust me, if there's one thing I'm not, it's gullible."

She glanced up at him appreciatively. "No, I would say you're probably not," she agreed with a breathy sigh. "You're being very broad-minded in letting us do this."

He shrugged, his remoteness not giving way before Courtland's practiced charm. "Lizzie wants it. It can't do any harm."

"Spoken like a man," Courtland said wryly. "Come with me, Lizzie. I need you to fill me in on a few things."

"So you can come across sounding knowledgeable?" Damien didn't move from his spot in the bedroom door.

"I'm not getting anything out of this, buddy," Courtland said, finally ruffled. "I'm just trying to help a friend."

Lizzie caught her arm and tugged her over to the sofa. "What do you want to know?"

"Is he always this charming?" Courtland grumbled.

"Sometimes he's even worse."

The blonde glanced toward the open bedroom door, through which Damien disappeared, and there was an appraising gleam in her eye. "Still, he's damned cute. I wouldn't kick him out of bed for eating crackers. I assume you two don't have anything going?"

Lizzie didn't blush, which was a wonder. She managed to keep her expression cool. "Why do you ask?"

"Because I don't poach on my friends' property if I can help it. If you're sleeping with him, I'll keep my distance.

It would have been easy enough to say something. To tell Courtland to keep her roving eyes off Damien. But she couldn't say it. Besides, despite her friend's insistence that she didn't trespass, Lizzie had seen her do it countless times. Asking her not to wouldn't keep her away.

"I'm not sleeping with him," she said. "I don't have any claims on him."

"I didn't think so. It's not really your style. Still, there's something that feels a little . . ." She let the sentence trail off. "It's nothing, I suppose. I just wanted to check before I started something. Is he going to be resistant?"

Lizzie had thought her sense of humor had just about deserted her, but it bounced back unexpectedly. "To you, or to what we're doing?"

"We'll work on finding the answers for now," Courtland said cheerfully. "We'll get to me later."

"You're wasting your time."

"It's my time to waste. So what are we doing here? Tarot reading, the runes? I brought my crystals. . . ."

"I think you should do a past-life regression."

Even Courtland's usual cheeriness abated somewhat. "That's pretty tricky. Even dangerous, if the person doesn't know what she's doing. I usually let Hickory take care of those sorts of things. After all, he taught me almost everything I know."

"And you were his best pupil—the only one with a real gift, he said. You know what you're doing."

"Do you think it's something from a past life? Have you sensed anything?"

"Nothing," Lizzie said, knowing she was lying, though not quite sure why. "It's just a thought. He has dreams, visions, though he denies them. I was hoping you could find out where they come from."

"Yes, but what if we don't like where they come from? What if he turns out to be some kind of weirdo?"

"Then you bring him out of it—fast."

"Wouldn't the tarot be a lot easier?"

"Certainly. You could just handily come up with the right card—The Lovers, say—and go from there," Lizzie said in a sour voice.

Courtland's brow creased. "Are you sure you aren't interested in the man? Sexually, I mean? There's a first time for everything."

"Trust me, Courtland, it wouldn't be the first time. There's no such thing as a twenty-eight-year-old virgin in the state of California.

"Well, it's the first in my memory. Are you? Interested in him?"

She'd lied once; she wasn't about to do it again. "As a matter of fact, Courtland," she said, in a quiet, pleasant voice, "you'll keep your damned hands off him. He's mine. Always has been, always will be."

For a moment, Courtland looked startled. Then she let out a little trill of laughter. "Always?" she echoed. "I'm not sure if I believe in the concept. Maybe we should do the past-life regression on you."

"No, thank you," Lizzie said stiffly. "It's Damien I'm worried about."

"How the mighty have fallen!" Courtland said. "Don't worry, darling, I'll behave myself. If I were Julianne, I might not be so honorable. I suppose I can do a past-life regression. After all, it's not as if our current lives are going to intertwine." She delved into the canvas bag at her feet and pulled out a package wrapped in worn black velvet. She unwrapped it carefully, exposing a huge purple crystal. "Go get the guinea pig, Lizzie. I always like watching the skeptics struggle."

He was on the bed, lying there in the darkness, staring up at the ceiling. She stood there for a moment, watching, realizing that he hadn't snapped his denim shirt yet, the shirt she'd ripped open in a frenzy. His chest was smooth, muscled, and she wanted to climb on the bed and touch him, run her hands along his rib cage, put her mouth against his neck and taste him.

Such fantasies astonished her. Damien was a man who called to her on every level—physical, sexual, emotional and spiritual. Through panic and calm, through the ages, she could feel his pull, and she wanted nothing more than to climb on the bed with him and shut the world away.

"Courtland's ready," she said, in a deceptively cool voice. "If you are."

He turned to look at her, and even in the darkness she could see the brilliance of his glance. "'Keep your damned hands off him'?" he echoed.

She could feel color suffuse her face, but she stood her ground, even as she tried to think of some offhand remark. "I thought maybe a little protection was in order," she said.

He rose from the bed in one fluid movement. "Who needs protection? Courtland? Or me?"

"Take your pick," she said, turning to leave.

He moved with unerring swiftness, catching her arm and turning her around, pushing her up against the bedroom wall, next to the open door. In the room beyond, Courtland was humming under her breath, oblivious of the tension in the bedroom. Lizzie could feel the hardness of the wall behind her, the hardness of

Damien's body pressing her against it, holding her there.

"I'm yours, am I? Always?" he said, and there was no missing his bleak, self-mocking grin. "Lord, Lizzie, I only wish it were that simple."

She let her eyelids flutter closed as she absorbed the feel of him against her. She could feel the sudden increase in tension, the hissing intake of breath. "Damn you, Lizzie," he muttered under his breath.

She opened her eyes and smiled at him. "Only if you want me."

The feel of him against her hips left no doubt in her mind, despite the torment in his eyes. He pulled himself away from her, heading into the living room like a man facing his executioner, and Lizzie almost smiled.

Damien threw himself into a worn old chair and glowered at the unruffled Courtland. Lizzie simply took a seat on the floor beside him, cross-legged, waiting.

"There are other seats, Lizzie," Courtland pointed out.

"I know." Her voice was deceptively tranquil. For one thing, she had a very basic, biological need to be near Damien. For another, she had no idea what Courtland's psychic probing might reveal, and she wanted to be close by in case he needed her.

She wasn't afraid of what Courtland would elicit. What was frightening, terrifying, was the unknown. Even if what they discovered was unpleasant, it couldn't be any worse than uncertainty.

She'd watched Courtland often enough, so this time she concentrated on Damien. His dark eyes were full of mockery and contempt, and his mouth was twisted in a derisive smile. Courtland was used to derision. Within moments Damien's mocking dark eyes were blank, dazed, as he stared at her rough-cut crystal and listened to her voice.

"What do you see?" Courtland crooned in the singsong voice that never failed to make the skin on Lizzie's back crawl. "Look at your feet. What do they look like?"

"Feet," Damien said caustically, with just the faintest slur.

"Who are you?"

"You know who I am."

"What do you do for a living?"

"I'm a reporter." He sounded bored, as if he found these obvious questions exceedingly tedious. But his eyes were unfocused, and his voice echoed faintly, as if he were speaking from a long distance away. It sounded different from his usual deep drawl, but Lizzie couldn't quite define that difference.

"I know you're a reporter. Who do you work for?"

"Isn't that obvious?" he said. "I work for the *London Star*. I have for the last seven years."

Then Lizzie knew with sudden horror that the difference in his voice was his accent. It was now cool, clipped—and British.

"Do you like your job, Mr.—? What did you say your name was?" Courtland persevered, her voice gentle and non-threatening.

"It's all right, most days," he said. "And the name's Killian. James Killian."

"James Killian," Courtland said, in a hollow voice. "What year is it, James?"

"You know that as well as I do, missus. It's 1888. November. It's a time people aren't likely to forget, with the Ripper roaming the streets."

"You know about the Ripper, do you, James?"

"Haven't I been following his case?" Damien demanded, clearly outraged. "Haven't I been the first reporter at the scene of the crime at most of the murders? Haven't I taken photographs? Ghastly things." He shuddered, and Lizzie wanted to reach up and touch his hand. "I don't know which one was worst," he continued. "Polly Nichols was bad enough. Cathy Eddowes was a right heartbreaker. But I think it was Long Liz Stride that got to me. Lying there in the blood, that bag of cashews still clutched in her hand. According to the prossies I talked to, Liz loved her cashews. Probably would have faced death rather than give 'em up. Poor old tart." He shook his head. "And he didn't even get a chance to do his trick on 'er. Someone must have caught him in the act. That's why he was so bad with Cathy Eddowes, just a few hours later."

"You knew these women, James?"

"I knew Liz and Cathy. See, I been down in Whitechapel, at the Ten Bells pub, ever since the second murder. The first one was no big deal—whores get murdered all the time, either by their pimps or their customers or their girlfriends. But two of them, that made me start to wonder. The police were getting interested, too, and James Killian's a man to keep his eye on the police."

"So you've been watching?"

"I've been watching," he said. "And I'll tell you another thing. I'm going to catch that bleeder. I'm gonna nail him, just for the edification of the *Star*'s readers." He leaned forward, crafty and confiding. "He's been sending me letters, see. We printed some of them— nasty they were, talking about eating her liver and all. But I've kept the last one. My editor hasn't even seen it."

"Wouldn't it help the police?"

"Why should I help the police? I look after meself, you know, Mrs. Killian's little boy James. I'm not about to queer the scoop of my life."

"What do you mean?"

"He's going after another one. He told me, enough so's that I know who she is. I'm going to catch him in the act, I am."

"Aren't you afraid?"

"I have a gun, and I know how to use it. If need be, I'll blow his bloody brains out. It'll make me a hero. Sell a thousand copies of the paper."

Courtland glanced at Lizzie, a troubled expression on her face. "Help me here, Lizzie," she said softly. "I don't know enough about the original case to ask the right questions."

"Neither do I," Lizzie said helplessly. She looked up at Damien. He looked very different. Younger. Arrogant. Even downright cocky. And he looked eerily, impossibly familiar. "How many people has the Ripper killed?" she asked in a hesitant voice.

"Haven't you been reading the papers?" he demanded, plainly affronted.

"I have. I just don't usually read the *Star*."

"Bleedin' aristocrat," he muttered. "Four women. Polly Nichols, Annie Chapman, Cathy Eddowes and Liz Stride."

"What about the last one?" Lizzie said, certain Damien had told her of five.

"What last one? There aren't going to be any more. I've got my eye on Mary Kelly, and there's no way anyone's going to get to her."

Lizzie turned a horrified face up to Courtland's, and she shook her head.

"It's two months later, James," Courtland said gently. "It's January. Where are you?"

His voice was muffled, slurred. "Drunk."

"Where, James?"

"Ten Bells. I did what I was supposed to do. I took the photographs. There she was, what was left of her. On the bed. On the table, as well. Pieces of her, everywhere." His voice broke in something akin to a sob.

"Who, James?" Lizzie asked.

"Mary Kelly."

"Who killed her?" she forced herself to ask.

He looked down at her. She'd reached out to clutch his hands, and they were icy cold, bloodless beneath her grip. "I killed her," he said. "I killed Mary Kelly."

"You could have warned me," Courtland said, in a querulous voice. She was standing in the deserted hallway, beneath the bare light bulb that illuminated Damien's door.

"Warned you about what? You must have guessed this would have something to do with the Ripper."

"I didn't expect it to be quite so graphic. I just wish I hadn't had to pull him out of it so fast. I was afraid of what he might do. If only Hickory had been here. He wouldn't have panicked like I did."

"Does Damien remember what he said?"

"I imagine so. Unless he's got the kind of mind where he can blank things out that he finds unacceptable." She ran a hand through her thick mop of blond hair, and in the harsh light of the single bulb she looked strained, drawn.

"Do you think he was telling the truth?"

Courtland shrugged. "People don't usually lie when they're under hypnosis, unless the lie goes so deep it feels like the truth to them. If he says he killed Mary Kelly, then he probably did. I think you should call the police."

"And tell them what? That Damien committed a murder over a hundred years ago? I can just imagine what Adamson would say to that."

"I don't think you should stay here. There's something going on, more than I could discover. I don't think you're safe with him."

"If I'm not safe with him, then who can protect me? Obviously not the police—they haven't managed to do anything to stop the murders. I'd rather take my chances with Damien."

Courtland just stared at her, and a wry smile curved her perfect lips. "Oh, Lord, Lizzie, what a time to fall in love..." she said softly.

"Don't be ridiculous," Lizzie said hotly. "I've only known him a couple of days, and he's hardly the stuff dreams are made of."

"Depends on your dreams, Lizzie. You forget, I know you. You never were attracted to the straightforward type." Courtland reached out and put her arms around her, hugging her tightly. "It's more than a couple of days. You know it as well as I do. We should have done your past lives instead of his. You've never let me try it with you. It might have given us the answers."

Lizzie shook her head. "Forget it. I'm already feeling schizophrenic enough as it is. I know who I am. I'm Lizzie Stride. I just don't know which Lizzie Stride."

Courtland shook her head. "I don't think so."

"What do you mean?"

"I mean it's not that simple. Just because you have the same name doesn't mean you're the same person. There's more to it, more to you, than I can figure. I'm

going to go find Hickory and see what he makes of it."
She looked at Lizzie. "Take care of yourself, kid. If you
won't come back home with me, at least watch your
back. I can feel . . ." She pulled back, and suddenly her
beautiful face looked old and skeletal. "I can feel
death," she said in a hushed tone.

"Courtland . . ."

"I'm getting out of here," the blonde said, starting
down the deserted hallway. "If I were you I'd call
Adamson."

"Be careful out there," Lizzie called after her.

Courtland paused as she stepped into the elevator.
"It's morning already," she said brightly. "Don't you
worry about me—I'll be more than safe. Worry about
yourself." And the elevator doors creaked shut behind
her.

The light in the apartment was shadowed, eerie, in the
early dawn. Damien was still sitting in the chair, his long
legs stretched out in front of him, and Lizzie stood
there, watching him surreptitiously, turning over in her
mind Courtland's unsettling words.

She'd never been in love in her life. Naturally, she'd
thought she was, so long ago, but Mark's betrayal had
quickly shattered that romantic notion. And with
Freddy, she'd been hoping that a vague attraction might
blossom into something more intense. When it hadn't,
she'd simply given up on the idea. Better to live in
peaceful celibacy than to waste her time chasing after
mediocre relationships and the wrong sort of man.

If anyone was the wrong sort of man, John Ripley
Damien was the epitome of the idea. Tormented, dangerous, he had room in his life for only one thing. His
obsession with the Ripper. He'd warned her straight out

that he had nothing to offer her. And the more he warned her, the more drawn she was.

She should have spent her early twenties reading those silly books about women loving the wrong sort of man, instead of concentrating on her mask-making. She was certainly showing no sense at all in being attracted to a man who was so patently bad for her. It must date back to her insecure childhood, and her unhappy early experiences with romance.

Except it wasn't that easy to explain. She'd learned how to take care of herself over the years, to protect herself from pain and disillusionment. She took one look at Damien and saw all the trouble in the world, and she knew he might very well be far more dangerous to her peaceful existence than a butchering serial killer.

But she took a second look at Damien and she wanted to go to him, to touch him. She wanted to lie naked with him, to kiss his mouth; she wanted to draw his head down to her breasts and comfort him. She wanted to clean his apartment, and feed him; she wanted to make him laugh. She wanted to do all sorts of impossible, stereotypical female-lover types of things with him. She wanted to experience everything, love and pain and laughter. And, rational or not, she wanted all those things with him.

"We're going to have to go out," he said, his voice rusty in the darkened apartment. "I need cigarettes."

The prosaic statement was oddly reassuring. She wanted to go to him, touch him, but she was afraid to. She curled up on the sofa, watching him, her knees up to her chest. "Are you all right?"

He didn't answer her. "What did your flaky friend tell you?"

"She's not flaky."

"She's flaky as hell. All that past-life mumbo jumbo," he muttered, not meeting her eyes.

"Do you remember any of it?"

"Of course I do," he snapped. "I was stringing her along. James Killian, boy reporter for the London newspapers."

"You're telling me you were playing a game? You made it all up?" She clenched her arms around her legs, staring at him fixedly.

"What do you think?"

"I think you're too skeptical for your own good. I think she tapped into your past life, and it scared the hell out of you. Damien, what you might have done in another lifetime doesn't have anything to do with your life today."

"Doesn't it?" His voice was bitter.

"Tell me the truth. I brought Courtland over to help. If you're just going to hide away from what she found out..."

"I'm not hiding from anything," he snapped. "Particularly not the truth."

"Then tell me."

He shook his head, not in negation, but more in an effort to distance himself. He focused on a spot behind her head, and she knew with only a faint trace of discomfort that he was looking at her masks.

"So she hypnotized me," he said. "I'll admit to that. Hypnosis exists. And while I was hypnotized, the combination of recent events, the research I've done and her suggestions made me . . . imagine certain things. Like a dream."

"Tell me your dream."

"Go to hell."

She didn't even flinch. She climbed off the couch and sat on the floor again, at his feet. She didn't touch him, but she knew he could feel her presence. And she knew, without being certain how she knew, that she gave him comfort.

"Tell me your dream, Damien," she said again.

He looked down at her, out of bleak, dark eyes. "If I tell you, will you agree to leave Los Angeles?"

She didn't want to leave him. But she was asking for more than he was willing to give. She needed to offer something in return.

"If you want me to," she said.

They stared at each other in a silence that spoke more than words could have. "I want you to," he said. "Before it's too late for both of us."

CHAPTER ELEVEN

Damien leaned back in the chair, closing his eyes as if in pain. Lizzie waited, patient, letting him take his time. The lights were off in the apartment, except for the dim glow from the bathroom, and the postdawn shadows played across the floor in stark, geometric patterns.

His voice came from far away, distant, detached, eerily calm. But it was his voice, not the cockney brashness of Jack Killian. "It was a dream," he said, "and I was watching him. Hell, he didn't even look like me. He was about five-eight, light brown hair, side-whiskers and a mustache. A flashy dresser in a bright plaid suit, and he wore a diamond pinkie ring." He touched his own hand, in an automatic gesture, as if searching for the missing ring.

"He thought he was so damned smart. He was going to make his career, he thought, on the heels of the Ripper. He wrote the articles, he even took the photographs, and he started to become famous. It didn't matter to him that he was whipping the people of Whitechapel and Spitalfields into a vigilante frenzy. It didn't even matter that he started getting letters, dozens of letters, from people claiming to be the Ripper. Until he got the real thing.

"He knew it immediately, knew that it had come from the Ripper himself. Boasting. And instead of turning the letter over to the police, he published it first, knowing that he was interfering with one of the few leads the London police could work with.''

Damien tilted his head back, closing his eyes. ''Killian didn't care about a damned thing but making his way. He came from a poor family in Shepherd's Bush, and he was determined to better himself. When he saw the first victim, he went into an alleyway and threw up. By the time he photographed Cathy Eddowes, he didn't even flinch.'' His voice trailed off, and for a moment there was silence in the dimly lit room.

''He knew them,'' he said finally, opening his eyes to glance at her. ''The last three victims. Liz Stride, Cathy Eddowes and Mary Kelly. He'd taken to hanging out at the Ten Bells, hoping to catch a glimpse of the Ripper himself. All the victims were last seen at the pub, and it stood to reason that the Ripper had been there, too. So he started hanging out there, chatting up the hookers, charming them.

''And the damnable thing was, the Ripper picked the women Killian liked particularly. Oh, he hadn't slept with them—our boy was too fastidious for that. But Cathy Eddowes had a certain bawdy sense of humor that reached beyond his self-importance, and Liz Stride was a rather scattered old lush, with a fondness for cashews and violets. She was really quite sweet and motherly, and when they found her body he almost wept.

''But Mary Kelly was the worst. Killian wanted her. Half fancied himself in love with her. The Ripper sent him one last letter. It taunted him, told him he'd seen him with Mary. And that Mary would be the last.''

Damien shuddered, and Lizzie wanted to reach out, to put her arms around him to comfort him, but she didn't dare. She was afraid that if she moved, if she said a word, she would break his concentration, and he wouldn't finish telling the dream that haunted him.

His voice changed, not back to the earlier broad cockney, but to an accent somewhere in between. "I didn't give that note to the police," he whispered. "God knows why. I guess I thought I could catch the Ripper, stop him. I had a gun, and what good was a knife against a gun? I could keep Mary safe. She didn't like it on the streets, and if the two of us were able to expose the Ripper, she'd become famous. She'd have chances, opportunities, that the others wouldn't have. She wanted to be an actress, and she was pretty enough. So pretty." His voice faded for a moment.

"But I was wrong. Stupid, murderously stupid. And Jack was far too clever. She didn't make a sound, they said, after one brief cry. She must have been dead before he did those things to her. She would never know what he'd done. What I'd done. By failing her. By waiting too long."

As Lizzie watched, in shock, slow tears began to slide down Damien's lean, dark face. There was no expression of grief, of sorrow, just the tears, testifying to his pain.

Lizzie waited as long as she could. When it seemed apparent that he wasn't going to say anything more, she risked speaking. "What happened?"

He started, as if he'd forgotten she was there. He stared down at her, seemingly oblivious to the dampness on his face. "Killian had to photograph the scene of the crime. He couldn't very well refuse to, any more than he could turn in the letter at that late date. He'd be accused of obstructing justice, he'd lose his job, and, after all, he'd brought about Mary's death for the sake of his career, hadn't he? Silly to throw it away, after the price she'd paid. She would have agreed with him, if she'd still had a tongue.''

He shook back his long hair, and his expression was stark, emotionless, in contrast to the salty tracks of his silent tears. "No one ever found the Ripper. Mary Kelly was his last victim, and without ghoulish murders to report, Killian didn't have much success. He started drinking heavily, and he died two years later. Drowned, in the Thames.'' His voice trailed off. "They thought it was an accident, but it wasn't. He just couldn't live with himself any longer.''

"And that was you,'' Lizzie said. It was half question, half statement. "In a previous life.''

He seemed to rouse himself with an effort. "Don't be ridiculous. It was a dream. The power of suggestion. Of course I'd think I was a reporter in a previous life. Of course...''

She moved then, on her knees, confronting him, putting her hands on his thighs, staring up at him earnestly. "Why do you keep fighting it? Don't you see, that explains things? Explains your obsession. You were a reporter, involved with the murders over a hundred years ago, and you feel responsible, frustrated. In this lifetime, you need to make peace with the past. This time you have to save Mary Kelly. You have to find the Ripper and stop him.''

"I'm not able to save anyone,'' he said harshly. "Women keep dying.''

"You've saved me. Kept me safe.''

"So far.'' His smile was mocking, derisive. "How long do you think I'll manage that?''

"Long enough, I hope.''

He reached out and touched her, his long fingers threading through her thick hair. "Long Liz Stride," he murmured. "What about *your* destiny?"

"My destiny?"

"You think your name's a coincidence? What about the others? Eddowes isn't a common name, but he could probably find a Mary Kelly, a Polly Nichols, an Annie Chapman. But he hasn't gone after them. He's coming for you. Haven't you wondered why?"

"Why don't you tell me?"

"He wasn't able to mutilate Liz Stride. Someone must have interrupted him while he was at work. She was in one piece, her body untouched except for her cut throat. That was one reason why he was particularly savage with Cathy. He cut out her liver and sent part of it to Killian, you know. He said he ate the rest of it."

I won't get sick, Lizzie told herself faintly. "I thought Killian was a dream."

He closed his eyes for a moment, and he looked unutterably weary. "Hell, Lizzie, I don't know. I don't know what's truth and what's a dream, what happened last week or last century. I know I'm John Ripley Damien, reporter for the *Los Angeles Chronicle*, not James Killian of the *London Star*. I've done my share of evil, including watching Mary Kelly immolate herself when I could have stopped her. . . ."

"Not Mary Kelly," she said. "You said her name was Betty."

He stared at her in shock. "Oh, God," he said. "God." And he pushed her away, stumbling out of the chair and into the bedroom, slamming the door behind him.

Lizzie stood in the living room, uncertain what to do next. Part of her wanted to run out the door into the early morning streets and flag down the first taxi she could find, one that would take her to LAX and away from all this confusion.

She had the money now; Hickory had given her enough cash to get her across the state line, at the very least. But she didn't want to leave, not even if her life depended on it. If Damien made her, she would go. But only if he made her.

Because she was afraid to leave him. His torment ran so deep, through the decades and the lifetimes, that she didn't know what would happen to him if he was alone. And not knowing would drive her crazy.

She wasn't in love; the idea was absurd. But she had a need, a very real need, to save Damien. As much as he seemed to need to save her.

She moved back to the couch, stretching out on its lumpy length. While she wanted to go to Damien, something told her that he needed to be alone.

She was so tired, so very tired. She closed her eyes as the murky morning light grew around her. In the distance she thought she heard a faint sound, like a cry, one that was abruptly shut off. And then she slept.

It was dark when Damien awoke, dark and hot. Despite the torpor of the room, he was covered with a cold sweat of terror, one he refused to give in to. He glanced at the digital clock beside the bed. It read 6:33 p.m. He'd slept the day away, in a deep, dreamless state, and he'd slept alone.

His whole body ached when he rose from the bed. He felt as if he'd run a marathon, something he'd been capable of doing in better times. Exhausted, every muscle protesting, he wanted nothing more than to stand under a hot shower and let the water drown his pain, drown his memory.

By the time he finished, he felt marginally more human. He tied his long, wet hair behind his head, pulled on baggy jeans and an old T-shirt that had once been black but was now an indeterminate shade of gray, and opened the door to the living room. It was shrouded in darkness, an ominous, eerie darkness, and for a moment he stood there, feeling the panic.

He could see her, stretched out on the couch. Lying on her stomach, her red hair spread around her, and he knew, he just knew, that when he reached to turn her over he would look into dead, staring eyes, just above a slashed throat. And in her hand she would be clutching a bag of cashews.

He moved in a fog, in slow motion, telling himself he could stand it. He touched her shoulder beneath the fall of hair, and it was still warm, still resilient. She hadn't been dead for long.

He turned her gently, and the eyes that stared up at him weren't wide in death. They were dazed, sleepy, and there was no blood, no bag of cashews, no smell of butchery, but instead the faint flowery fragrance of her perfume. "Lizzie," he said, no longer able to keep the feeling out of his voice. "Lizzie," he said again, and pulled her into his arms.

She went sweetly, willingly, warm and fragrant and endearingly innocent, wrapping her arms around him, pulling his head down to her soft breasts, her breath hot against his hair. Suddenly she was everything to him, hope and despair, wife and mother and lover, child and enemy. He knew he was wrong to take her, and he knew nothing on this earth could stop him. Not in this lifetime, and not in any past lifetime.

He kissed her then, softly at first, nibbling at her lips, coaxing her. She stiffened in surprise, and he knew that one little moment of denial should stop him. And he knew it wouldn't.

He cupped her head with his hands, slanting his mouth across hers, and deepened the kiss, using his tongue to taste her, claim her. It had been so long, so damned long, since he had tasted love. Over a hundred years.

She clutched his shoulders with her hands, her strong artist's hands, and he could feel her giving in, falling into acceptance, eagerness, delight. Her tongue touched his, sliding against his, and he could feel the rapid pounding of her heart through their combined clothing.

He broke the kiss, staring down at her in the murky twilight. "Come to bed with me," he said.

"Yes." There wasn't the slightest fear or hesitation in her voice.

He scooped her up in his arms, effortlessly, and carried her into the bedroom, laying her down on the bed, following her down, covering her body with his as his mouth traced random patterns over her eyelids, her cheekbones, the fragile beauty of her ear. She was soft and warm beneath him, rounded hips against his lean ones, long legs entwined with his, breasts pushing against the cloth of the shirt she wore so that he could feel her nipples in the darkness.

He sat back, straddling her, watching her as he began to unfasten the small buttons. Her face looked dazed, wary, her mouth soft and bruised, and he wanted to lose himself in her mouth, her body. His hands grew clumsy, impatient, and he ripped open the rest of her shirt, knowing he'd done this before.

She had beautiful breasts, small and perfectly formed. He leaned over and put his mouth on her, drawing the nipple deep and hard against his tongue, and her body jerked in reaction. Her hands were clutching the rumpled sheet beneath them, and he pulled one away, bringing it to the front of his jeans, holding it there, feeling the exquisite agony of a desire so strong he didn't know how long he could make it last.

He could feel the darkness closing around him, could feel the blood beating in his ears. His hands were rough as they stripped off her jeans, but if she protested he was beyond hearing, lost in some black, dangerous place of his own. He could taste blood when he kissed her, and it fed his appetite, as if he were some crazed vampire. He stripped off his own clothes, and when she tried to reach for him, to put her arms around him, to slow him down or to stop him, to protect him or to kiss him, he wouldn't let her, catching her wrists and holding them down on the mattress as he positioned himself between her legs.

He could feel darkness and death all around, and he thrust into her, deep, hearing and ignoring her small cry of protest. She wasn't ready, and he didn't care, he simply wanted to take her, take her, to thrust into her body again and again.

And suddenly he could see the knife in his mind's eye, thrusting, bloody, sexual, and he made a hoarse cry, one of pain, of despair, forcing his body to still within the tight, hot depths of hers.

He was still achingly aroused, damn his soul. He lifted his head and looked down at her, saw the shock and hurt and fear in her dark eyes. He wanted to calm her, to reassure her, to tell her he was sorry, but there were no words to answer that look in her eyes.

And he was still hard, damn it. Her mouth was bleeding from the force of his, and he brushed his lips against hers, so gently that she couldn't have responded even if she'd wanted to. And then he kissed her eyelids closed, seeing with a distant kind of horror that he left traces of her own blood on her lids.

He angled his body up, reaching between them to touch her, and her deathlike stillness evaporated as she struck at him, trying to push him away.

"No," she said fiercely. "Don't. I don't want you to touch me...."

He wasn't going to listen to her, and neither was her body. Despite her hurt and anger, she was aroused, and he was deft, determined, as he made her climax, her body tightening and rippling around his aching hardness, as a helpless little cry filled the darkness.

It would have taken nothing at all to push him over the edge, to follow her. A sigh, a whisper, the stroke of her hand on his arm. He kept himself very still, waiting until the last tremor died away from her body, the last stray shiver passed over her skin. Waited until the tears stopped seeping from beneath her closed lids.

And then he pulled away, out of her, pushing off from the bed, moving to the bathroom and slamming the door behind him, locking it.

He stared at his reflection in the mirror. At the haggard face, at the arousal that mocked. And then he turned on the shower, full blast, and stepped in, letting the icy-cold water sluice down around him. Wishing it would drown him.

Lizzie grabbed one of the pillows and hugged it tightly against her body. She was still frightened, still shaken, still more confused than she'd been in her entire life.

He'd hurt her. And yet, for the first time in her life, she'd climaxed. And he had been the one to make her do it.

She hated him for that. She could have endured the pain, the degradation. She had before. But after terrifying her, shutting down her reactions with his brutality, he'd made her come alive again, more alive than she'd felt in her entire life, and she would never forgive him.

And she was frustrated, because he hadn't finished. He'd left her, after bringing her to an unwilling climax, and she felt empty, unfinished, needful. She cursed herself for feeling that way. For the sheer illogic of it.

She lay alone in the darkness, shivering despite the heat. It had stopped raining. She was so used to the constant drizzle that the very absence of it was intrusive, startling.

The two doors leading from the bedroom were closed, shutting her within the sultry darkness. She could hear the sound of the shower, and she knew she should pull on her clothes and run from this place, from this man.

But he'd slammed the door to the living room when he'd carried her to bed like some romantic lover and then proceeded to terrify her and hurt her. And she didn't want to get up and open that door.

She wasn't sure why. She just had this deep, dreadful sense that whatever lay beyond the living room door was too horrifying to face. Better to face the fear she knew, the face of John Ripley Damien than to open the door on a darkness deeper than any she'd ever known.

She pulled the sheet up over her body, wrapping it around her, still clutching the pillow in place of someone's warm, loving body. She felt shaken, frightened, hurt. And just once, just for a moment, she would have liked to feel peace.

It seemed like hours before she heard the shower turn off, hours longer before the door to the bathroom opened, flooding the dark bedroom with a harsh glare. Lizzie allowed herself a small, sullen glance at Damien as he stood in the doorway. He was dressed, at least partially, in a pair of baggy jeans that had probably once fit him. His hair was wet, he'd shaved, and his expression, as usual, was blank.

"I was afraid you might have run," he said, reaching for one of the shirts she'd dumped on the nearby chair. It was a black T-shirt, and for a moment she started, fascinated, as he pulled it on. It had the skull-and-roses Grateful Dead logo emblazoned across the front.

"Don't wear that shirt," she snapped, still hugging the pillow, refusing to meet his eyes.

He glanced down at it, then pulled it back over his head, tossing it into the wastebasket. "Did I hurt you?"

"I don't want to talk about it," she muttered into the pillow, closing her eyes, trying to close him out.

She felt the bed sag beneath his weight, and she stiffened, afraid he would touch her, afraid she would let him. But he remained where he was, until she warily opened her eyes.

"Did I hurt you?" he asked again, calm, patient, inexorable.

She thought about it for a moment, not interested in sparing his feelings. She almost considered lying, then thought better of it. "No," she said.

"Are you sure?"

She raised her head at that, finally goaded beyond endurance, beyond embarrassment. "For crying out loud!" she snapped. "If I said no, I meant it! Do you think I'm in the mood to spare your tender feelings? It was a little uncomfortable, okay?"

"I'm sorry," he said.

"Oh, for God's sake," she said. "Could we just drop it? So we made a mistake. I'm used to it. You told me to leave you alone, that you had nothing to give me, and I didn't listen. I never had good taste when it came to men. You've probably pointed that out to me. Just chalk it up as one more bad error in judgment and leave it—"

He hauled her into his arms and kissed her, effectively silencing her tirade, and his mouth was so sweet, so gentle against hers, that she wanted to start crying all over again. "It's not your fault," he murmured against her cheek. "It's mine. Something came over me, something horrible. It scared me, and I was afraid I might hurt you." He cupped her face, looking down at her, and for a moment his emotions were no longer masked, and he looked real and lost and infinitely dear.

"Damien," she breathed, wanting to kiss him again.

He shook his head, pulling away from her. "You believed what Courtland told you, didn't you?"

The abrupt change in subject startled her. "Yes," she said. "Did you?"

He didn't answer, simply moved to the door, staring at it in surprise, as if he hadn't remembered closing it. "I don't know," he said. "But I think I'd better warn you about something."

"I've been warned about enough things."

He paid no attention to her protest. "Just because I wasn't Jack the Ripper in a previous life," he said, "that doesn't mean I'm not him in this one." And he opened the living room door and left her without another word.

CHAPTER TWELVE

It was a simple enough matter to break into the abandoned apartment. He stood beneath the shower, washing the blood from his body, scrubbing it from beneath his fingernails. He'd worn a raincoat, but his shoes were a mess, and even his hair was matted with the stuff.

It would be much easier if he could do his work naked. Then he wouldn't have to worry about getting the errant stains out of his clothes.

Not in this lifetime, he thought sadly, stepping out of the shower and looking at his reflection in the filthy mirror. He squinted, and the form altered its shape, moving, coalescing, changing from a lithe, strong bodybuilder with close-set eyes and flowing blond hair to a paunchy, middle-aged bureaucrat. He blinked, and it shifted again, to a woman, soft and rounded, and he felt the blood lust rise in him once more. And then his vision cleared, and he could see himself as most people saw him. Ordinary. Harmless.

It was a gift he'd been given. The ability to project whatever he wanted when the killing haze was upon him. It was no wonder he was never recognized. No wonder he'd gotten away with it, in this lifetime and so many others.

He dressed quickly. His shoes were wet, the cheap imitation leather soaked where he'd scrubbed the blood away. His socks were wet, as well, and uncomfortable.

In a matter of moments he was back again, himself, a decent man who wouldn't harm a fly. He picked up the package, tucking it under his arm with extreme care, and started toward the bathroom door. He paused, turning back, and met his eyes in the mirror, eyes that were shifting and rainbow colored.

He looked into those kind, worried eyes, and he laughed softly.

The living room was ablaze with light when Lizzie came out of the bedroom. Damien had turned on every single lamp, and he was standing at the picture window, staring out over the city, his shoulders hunched, tense, a glass of pale liquid in one hand.

Lizzie paused, staring about her, uneasy. Something wasn't right about the room, she'd felt it ever since she'd lain in bed, watching the closed door, but she couldn't figure out what.

He turned at the sound of her footsteps, and there was no reading the expression on her face. "You found something to wear," he said.

"Yes." She tugged at the oversize T-shirt, then regretted her action as his eyes immediately went to her breasts. In the heat of the room, the heat of his gaze, she felt her nipples harden, and she quickly crossed her arms across her chest like a self-conscious adolescent.

"I wasn't thinking about your breasts," he said wryly. "But I am now." He turned away, looking out into the night. The rain had started again, a light drizzling, coating the cracked window and running down in rivulets. "Do you want a drink? There's some tequila left. No, that's right, you hate tequila." He took a long, meditative drink from his own glass. "All the more for me."

She reached out to touch him, putting her hand on his bare arm, and he jerked away, as if burned, and the liquor sloshed over the carpet.

"Don't," he said in a tight voice. "Don't touch me. Don't come near me."

She didn't move. "Why?"

"Haven't you been paying attention here, Lizzie? Keeping score? I could have hurt you tonight. Hell, I could have killed you. Something came over me. I don't know what it was. Memories, dreams. Maybe I was possessed by demons. Maybe I was possessed by something else. Just be glad I stopped in time. Before you were hurt even worse."

All her anger and hurt had vanished, leaving behind only a raw, aching wound. She wanted to touch him, heal him, drive those demons away from him. All she could do was stand there. "You didn't hurt me," she said.

"I could have. Damn it, don't you understand? I don't know where it would have stopped. You might have ended up in pieces all over the bedroom, just like Mary Kelly...."

"I thought I was Long Liz Stride."

"It's nothing to joke about."

She managed a very small smile. "No." She reached out to him again, and he whirled around, twisting his arm to catch hers.

"Don't," he said again. "Or I'll take you back into the bedroom, and God only knows how it will end. We might not even get that far. Stop looking at me like that, Lizzie, or I swear I'll tear the clothes off your body and take you right here on the floor."

"I wouldn't stop you."

He groaned. "Haven't you learned anything, Lizzie?"

"Yes. I learned I'm in love with you."

He caught her other arm, pulling her up to him. He was still hard with wanting her. "Damn it, Lizzie," he muttered, his head moving down to hers, when suddenly he stopped.

She felt the horror suffusing his body as his gaze focused past her shoulder and his fingers tightened on her arms. "What is it?" she asked in a hushed voice.

"The masks," he said. "They're gone."

He released her, and she turned, looking at the wall where the two masks had hung. They were gone; the wall was bare. Except for a streak of rusty brown, where the clown mask had hung.

"When?" Lizzie managed to gasp.

"They were there when we got here," he said. "They were there when I carried you into the bedroom."

Lizzie shoved her fist into her mouth to stop the scream that threatened to erupt. And then he caught her hand, yanking her toward the door. "We're getting out of here," he said. "Now."

"What if he's still in the building?"

"Then he can get in here, despite my security. He's already proved it. We're getting the hell out of Venice, out of L.A. entirely. We're going to drive as far and as fast as we can. Come on, damn it!" he said, hauling her through the door.

The hallway was deserted, the bare light bulb swaying slightly for no reason whatsoever. And then Lizzie's eyes focused on the brown streaks along the wall. "Damien," she whispered.

"Don't look," he said. "Just come with me." He jammed the button of the elevator, and a loud buzzing noise could be heard coming from the shaft. "Damn," he muttered, turning and heading back the other way, through the bloody hallway, shoving open the metal door to the stairway.

Lizzie held back for a brief, horrified moment. "He might be down there."

"No elevator, Lizzie," he said, jerking her.

"It's coming," she said, listening to the creak of the old lift as it rose upward.

"Come with me, Lizzie. You don't want to be any-where near that elevator."

She didn't listen. She pulled away, and started back down the hallway, just as the elevator door slid open with a wheezing sigh. "There's no one in there," she called over her shoulder. "Come on, Damien, we can—"

And then she saw her. What was left of her. The floor of the elevator was awash with blood, the corpse of the woman lying there so mutilated and disfigured that Lizzie could barely recognize it as having once been human. In the middle lay the mask of the clown, mat-ted with blood. She stood there in the open door to the elevator, frozen in space and time.

She didn't even feel Damien put his arms around her, drawing her away. Time passed in a blur as she fought to keep from screaming. She shut down everything, her vision, her mind, her sense of smell, moving where Damien led her, a shell with no life with which to feel pain.

And then it left her, that hard cocoon of safety, and she was in the front seat of Damien's car, speeding away from the city as the rain beat down around them. She had no idea how much time had passed since they left the apartment—it could have been minutes, it could have been days.

She began to shake so hard that she thought her bones would fall apart. "Don't," he said, glancing at her out of the corner of his eye. "Don't remember, don't think about it, or it will haunt you."

"Do you think I have any choice in the matter?" she cried, her voice a raw whisper of pain. "Oh, God, Damien, that poor woman..."

"Stop it, Lizzie," he snapped. "There's nothing you can do for her now. Take what comfort you can in the fact that she would have felt very little."

"How do you know?"

"There have been enough autopsies, and I've read every one. He cuts their throats, and they're usually dead before he goes on to the more creative aspects of his—"

"Stop it!" It was no whisper, it was a scream, and the violence of it was shocking. "Stop it," she said again, in a quiet voice this time. She looked around her. "You're going the wrong way."

"What do you mean?"

"I want to go to my apartment."

"Lizzie, you're not safe. I won't leave you there alone. We're getting the hell away from here, and we'll call the police when we stop."

"I don't want you to leave me," she said. "I need to get something."

"What?"

"The masks. I'm not going to leave them for him to get his hands on. If he runs out of masks, he'll run out of killing."

"I don't think it's going to be that simple."

"It's the only thing I can do, Damien," she said, in a dull voice. "Grant me that much."

"What if he's waiting at your apartment? Waiting for you? That body in the elevator wasn't a random choice. It was a message for you."

"Maybe he thought it *was* me."

Damien shook his head. "He's not going to make any more mistakes." He jerked the wheel savagely, and the car slid on the wet surface as he turned back.

She was out of the car the moment he pulled up outside her apartment, and he managed to get ahead of her only by sprinting, stopping her at the door and barring the way. "Let me check first," he said. "He doesn't kill men."

Lizzie looked down at the doorknob in horror. "Damien," she whispered, "someone's been here."

Damien pushed the door open slowly, stepping into the dark interior of the apartment, and Lizzie was right behind him. She could see the outlines of her masks against the walls, and her relief was enormous. Until she saw the shadow of a man against the window, eerily motionless.

It was him, she thought dazedly. The Ripper had found her, and it was too late to run. And all she could think was that she wished Damien had finished what he'd started with her, just a short while ago.

"Run, Lizzie," Damien said under his breath.

But Lizzie was frozen, staring at the figure in her apartment as it slowly turned toward them, expecting to look into the yawning gates of hell.

Damien's arm shot out, and he turned on the light, flooding the room. Illuminating the hunched-over figure of Hickory, his straggly gray hair loose around his face, his expression an unreadable one.

The terror left Lizzie in such a rush that she almost collapsed. "Hickory!" she cried, starting toward him, when Damien reached out a hand to stop her.

"You're too trusting, Lizzie," he said in a cool voice.

"Don't be ridiculous. Hickory isn't the Ripper," she said angrily, trying to shake off his grip.

"No," said Hickory. "I have neither the strength nor the dexterity." And he held up his hands, hands that were gnarled and distorted by the crippling arthritis that had plagued him for most of his adult life. There was no way he could wield a knife with surgical precision.

Damien cursed, released Lizzie, and shut the door behind them, shutting out the rain and the night and the darkness. "Then what the hell are you doing here?" he demanded. "And how did you get in?"

"I have Courtland's key." His voice sounded ancient, sepulchral. "I was looking for you, Lizzie. So are the police. There's been another murder."

"I know," she said in a dull voice. "We saw her...or what was left of her. We were just at the apartment..."

"We left my place two hours ago, Lizzie," Damien said, moving past her and starting to take the masks down from the wall. She had a wicker basket, filled with artfully arranged branches and pine cones. He dumped them on the floor and began to place the masks inside.

"Don't be ridiculous. It was only a few minutes...."

"You were in shock, Lizzie," Damien said. "It's after one in the morning."

Lizzie ignored the unacceptable, turning to Hickory. "Why were you looking for me, Hickory?" she asked.

"I was looking for both of you. I have two reasons."

Damien had the child mask in his hands, and his touch was gentle, absently caressing, as he stared at the old man. "Why?"

"Time has run out. You don't want the answers now, but I can't count on being around to give them to you later."

"Bull," Damien said, wrapping that particular mask in a soft afghan before reaching for another.

"Tell us, Hickory," Lizzie pleaded, throwing an admonishing glare over her shoulder at the stubborn Damien.

Hickory moved across the room in a shuffle. He looked old, and weary beyond death. "I know what you fear, young man," he said to Damien, and Damien halted in his packing, a distrustful expression on his face.

"You've been talking to Lizzie's flaky friend Courtland," he said accusingly.

"No," Hickory said, and his voice held an ageless sorrow that sent chills through Lizzie. "Though I taught her everything she knows. But I know what she knows. I know about your past life, Damien. And I know about your present karma."

"And you're going to enlighten me," Damien drawled. "What are you going to want in return?"

"That you take care of Lizzie. Keep her safe. There's been too much death," Hickory said, in a voice that sounded like a funeral march.

"I'm already doing that. Okay, old man. Tell me my karma." He folded his arms across his chest, looking skeptical.

"You were a reporter in your most recent past life. A man named James Killian, who worked for a tabloid, a man who let the woman he loved die because he was too intent on getting a story. You've been paying for that ever since."

"You and Courtland must have cooked that one up between you," he drawled.

"Stop it, Damien," Lizzie said sharply. "Don't try to pretend you don't recognize what he's saying."

Damien scowled at her. "Okay," he said. "I'll humor you. So I let Mary Kelly die instead of saving her. It was a mistake. Morally reprehensible, but not a crime."

"You drowned yourself a couple of years later, when you couldn't drink yourself to death fast enough," Hickory said, and there wasn't a trace of censure in his voice. "That's why you didn't come back for such a long time. Suicides don't reincarnate right away."

"Oh, spare me," Damien snarled.

"But you did come back. You came back to expiate the sins of your past life. But what did you do? You stood by and watched another woman die, and did nothing about it."

All of Damien's false boredom vanished. "Shut up, old man," he said furiously.

"But that still doesn't make you the Ripper," Hickory continued, unmoved. "That's why you're here. To stop him this time. To save Mary Kelly. You've almost failed, and you're paying the price for it. You see what he does, but not in time to stop him. The only way you can turn off those bloody visions is to kill the Ripper."

Damien was no longer making any pretense at skepticism. "Damn you," he said. "Mary Kelly's dead. It's too late."

"Not in this lifetime," Hickory said. "Are you so blinded by the Ripper that you can't see what's in front of your eyes? She's not Long Liz Stride. Lizzie isn't the reincarnation of some cheerful old drunk—life isn't that simple. She's Mary. And this time you have to save her.''

"No," Lizzie said, in a horrified voice. "I'm not."

Hickory's lined old face was infinitely sorrowful. "I can't change it, Lizzie. Only Damien can."

"How the hell can I fight what I don't understand?" Damien said, the cynicism vanishing for a moment, leaving only pain and despair.

"Only you have the power. You're not fighting a man. You're fighting an entity, a source of evil, who takes over a man's body to do his work. You have to kill him, Damien. Kill the man he possesses. If you fail, he'll escape in this lifetime, and he'll come back in other lives to kill again."

Damien hoisted the basket overflowing with masks and started toward them, and his dark face had once more closed down into blank planes of disbelief. "Come on, Lizzie. Let's get the hell out of here. And if I were you, old man, I'd take your fantasies back to your buddy Courtland, and the two of you can have a wonderful time together."

"I expect I'll be seeing her shortly," Hickory said, and there was something in his voice that stopped Lizzie as she started after Damien.

"Why did you come here, Hickory? You said you had two reasons?"

"Little Flame," Hickory said, in a slow, sad voice, "it wasn't just anyone they found in the elevator at Damien's building. Courtland never came home."

Lizzie sat next to him in the car, her face white as death, her hands clenched in her lap. She hadn't spoken a word since Hickory had told her it was Courtland in the elevator. She'd gone out to the car ahead of Damien, sat passively as he closed her door, then got in the car himself. And then he'd taken off into the night like a bat out of hell, not giving a damn if the police, the National Guard or the president himself wanted to find them.

He knew where he was taking her, and he would have told her if she'd been able to ask. But she'd closed down tighter than she had before, shutting out everything, locked in her own private hell. And he could only hope she found some comfort there. He'd long ago lost any chance of comfort.

Damn that old man! Damn his eerie words. Lizzie had already been spooked enough; she hadn't needed to hear that it was her best friend who'd been butchered. Killed because she'd come to help them.

And she didn't need to hear that her own fanciful role in all this was far more complex than anyone could have imagined. *Was* she the reincarnation of Liz Stride or Mary Kelly? Or some weird, deadly combination of the two?

And what the hell stupid kind of question was that for him to be considering? He didn't believe in reincarnation. He didn't believe in a damned thing except staying alive for as long as he possibly could. And, even more important, keeping Lizzie alive.

So maybe it made kind of weird sense. He'd let her die once before, and then he'd gone and done the same thing again, letting another woman die while he searched for a story, a sound bite. Maybe he needed to save Lizzie, whoever she was, to expiate his sins.

And maybe he was getting just as crazy as Hickory. Just as crazy as the Ripper himself. All he knew was that when he'd looked into the elevator it had been something he'd already seen. Far too many times.

The farther he drove from the L.A. city limits, the clearer the weather was. He was heading southeast, into the desert, looking for dry air and sunshine. With his luck, he would simply find more Santa Ana winds.

The Ripper had found them in West Covina. Would he find them in the desert?

He hadn't been back there in so damned long. Back to the small desert town where he'd grown up with an elderly, embittered mother. His father had died in a car crash not long after he was born; his much-older brother had died in the first years of the Vietnam escalation, and Damien and his mother had lived together in that huge old Victorian house on the outskirts of town, alone, secluded.

He'd escaped as often as he could, involving himself in any kind of extracurricular activity he could find at the local high school. He'd never been particularly social, but his need to escape had overpowered his isolationist tendencies. He had thrown himself into track and baseball, the school paper and the debating society, anything that would keep him away from that house and the bitter old woman who lived there.

She wasn't there anymore. She'd developed Alzheimer's disease when he was in journalism school, and he'd put her in a nursing home when he could no longer find people to stay with her. She'd died alone, when he was overseas on a story, and by the time he'd returned to the desert town she was already buried, next to his father and brother. He could only hope she was happy at last.

He'd closed up the old house, thinking he would fix it up sooner or later, maybe sell it. But all he'd done was forget about it, hoping it might fall into the desert so that he would never have to think about it again.

But he suspected that it hadn't fallen apart. Suspected that the earthquakes had left it alone, that the rains and high winds had spared it. It would still be there, bleak, forlorn, inviolate. A living testament to his mother's lonely spirit. And his own.

No one would find them there. They could camp out for a few days, just until things settled down. The people of southern California were out for blood, and Adamson would have to find the Ripper, sooner or later. But he would damned well have to do without Damien's help, and without using Lizzie as a decoy.

He glanced behind him into the small back compartment of the Austin-Healey. The wicker basket of masks had toppled over, and the mask of the child was lying there, unwrapped.

It shook him. The moment he'd seen it, that mask had shaken him to the core. He'd looked at that mask, with all its innocence, pain and vulnerability, and fallen in love. Not with the child, but with the stubborn, beautiful woman who'd made it, who'd worn that face in her childhood.

He'd known that face, and the vulnerable soul it exposed. Known her and loved her in this life. And in the past. She seemed to be asleep, amazingly enough. He could hear the steadiness of her breathing, but her fists were still clenched, and even as she slept he could see that she was strung out with tension. She'd been through too much, and he wished to God there was some way he could spare her. He was doing the best he could, taking her to the one place he could think of where no one could find them.

But even that wasn't enough. Sooner or later the Ripper would find them. And if Hickory was right, sooner or later he himself would have to expiate his sin.

Or watch Lizzie die.

CHAPTER THIRTEEN

He'd lost her. Lost them both. How could it have happened, when he'd been so close, so very close, to finishing it? The woman had been a nice touch—she'd known him when she looked into his eyes, known who and what he was. She'd had time to scream, just once, before he'd cut her throat. But her eyes had kept staring at him as he used his knife, until he couldn't stand it any longer, and when he'd finished with her he'd put the mask over what had once been her face.

He was running out of time. He must have just missed them in the old building, and by the time he reached her apartment, they had already been and gone. He stumbled on her front step, crashing through the door, only to find the wall empty. There were no more masks.

He stood, desperate, bereft, and then someone moved. A figure detached itself from the far wall, and the old man moved into the light.

He knew that man. He was one of those who called themselves righteous, a sorcerer who could see too much, and he was staring at him as if he knew. As if he knew as much as that woman had known, just before he'd killed her.

He told himself not to panic. He hadn't thought he needed to change. People who knew him were less likely to have their vision clouded, and while he planned to finish with Lizzie Stride tonight, he wanted it on his terms. He didn't want to be forced into doing it clumsily.

The old man was looking at him with knowing eyes, and he had to remind himself that he had a perfectly logical explanation for being there. He had only the one mask left—it was all he needed for Long Liz Stride. He couldn't afford to waste it on a nosy old man.

"What are you doing here?" the old man demanded in a fearless voice.

He ignored the question. "Where are they? Where did they go?"

He expected instant obedience. Instead, the old man's face set in stubborn lines. "Not in this lifetime," he said.

He moved closer. He'd washed the knife when he'd finished with the woman, and now it lay tucked up inside his sleeve, waiting to be used. He was going to have to; he knew it. He was going to have to take his first man. He might even find himself developing a taste for it.

"Tell me, old man," he whispered, grabbing him by his seamed throat. "Before I cut your tongue out."

Slowly Hickory shook his head, grim defiance in his pale eyes. And then there was nothing but amazement as the killer brought the knife up, into the old man's belly, and twisted it.

It was midmorning when Damien started down the road to his mother's abandoned house. Even twenty years ago no one else had lived out that far, and while civilization had begun to encroach on the desert community, the mobile homes had gone up on the other side of town, leaving the old Victorian house with no neighbors, no witnesses. He pulled up behind the building, then killed the engine. Lizzie slept on, oblivious, and he almost hated to wake her.

The ancient Austin-Healey hadn't come equipped with air-conditioning, and the morning sun was baking down, turning the car into an oven. His mother's house had no air-conditioning, either, though if he was lucky, he might find an old electric fan up in the attic. That is, if the electricity worked.

He paid the bills regularly, but in the past few months he'd tended to let practical matters slide. For all he knew, they could have turned the power off.

They would find out soon enough. And by nightfall they would need a heater more than they would need cooling now. This part of California was merciless this time of year—desperately hot beneath the bright sun, bitterly cold once the sun went down.

He reached out a hand and touched her face, sliding his fingers beneath her thick fall of hair. She jerked awake, startled, and stared into his eyes in silent panic.

"We're here," he said gently.

"Where?"

It was the first word she'd spoken since they'd left her apartment, left Hickory, and her voice sounded distant, strained. "My mother's house. It's on the outskirts of a small town in the California desert."

She glanced around her, her brown eyes flat and incurious. "I didn't know you had a mother."

"Most people do. Mine's long dead. All my family's gone."

"Then the house is yours."

He shrugged. At least she was making a marginal amount of sense. "I suppose so. Somehow, I think it's always going to be my mother's house." He couldn't keep the trace of bitterness out of his voice, but Lizzie didn't seem to notice.

"How long are we staying?" she murmured, fumbling with the door handle with stiff, awkward fingers.

"As long as we need to."

"Until the Ripper finds us?"

"He won't find us. No one will. Even Adamson doesn't know where we went. I shook off at least two unmarked cars that tried to tail us, and for the last two hours I haven't seen anyone on the road."

"But they'd know about this place."

"No. It's not listed in my name. I haven't been here in over ten years. No one who knows me is even aware of its existence. We'll be safe here. At least for a while."

She just looked at him. There was no skepticism in her face, in her warm brown eyes. Just flat acceptance of an impossible fate. "All right," she said, opening the door.

"Damn it, Lizzie, I won't let him get you," he said, running a hand through his wind-tangled hair.

Her smile was small, distant, and heartbreaking. "I don't think you're going to have any say in the matter. You heard Hickory. Our past lives are catching up with us. You have the sins of this lifetime and your last one to make up for. I don't get to be just one of Jack the Ripper's original victims—I'm a combination of two of them. Nothing's going to save me. You're going to watch me die, Damien. And there won't be a damned thing you can do about it."

She climbed out of the car, standing in the barren, windswept backyard of the house he'd grown up in. She was tall, graceful, strong, with those long, wonderful legs of hers. She looked like a martyr going to the stake, and he wanted to take her strong shoulders in his hands and shake her.

He reached for the basket of masks and climbed out, walking past her up the rickety back stairs. The Santa Ana winds were blowing, hot and angry, swirling around the house, whipping up the dirt in the grassless yard. How many autumns had he spent in that house, trying to escape? And why in God's name had he returned, looking for a haven in what had once been his prison?

The key worked easily enough, and the damp, unused smell of the house washed over them when he pushed the kitchen door open. It smelled of dust and dead air, of wasted lives and lost dreams. He dumped the basket on the kitchen table and headed for the window, shoving it open. The hot desert air burst into the kitchen with the force of the winds, bringing in the sand, stirring the grit that coated every surface.

He turned to Lizzie. "Aren't you going to start in with me? Ask me where the vacuum cleaner's kept?" He flicked the light switch, and nothing happened. "Cancel that. Guess you're going to have to make do with a broom, at least until I see what I can do about the electricity. Maybe I can haul a few buckets of water for you to start scrubbing."

He couldn't get even a trace of response from her. "I don't care," she said, turning her back on him, wandering into the shadowed hallway.

He watched her go, tight with frustration. Sexual frustration, pure and simple, the obvious aftermath of having been sheathed in the glorious milking tightness of her body and then pulling free, refusing himself the release she'd offered. And emotional frustration. Lizzie had been angry, funny, mocking and charming. The emotions that had churned through her had brought him back to life. To watch her shut down was almost more painful than death.

She'd disappeared into the shadowy darkness, and he gave in to a momentary panic, one that faded once he considered it. The only monsters haunting this old house were the ghosts of his childhood. This lifetime, not a past one. And the sooner he saw about fixing up some electricity, the better off they would be. For a house in the middle of the sun-washed desert, it was a dark, gloomy old building, and he wanted to fill it with as much light as he could.

In the end, it was simple. Someone, maybe Damien himself, had thrown the main breaker when they'd left. When he switched it back, a faint hum filled the house as the refrigerator chugged back into fretful life.

He'd stopped at a local convenience store on his way into town, grabbing the necessities of life while Lizzie slept on—if, indeed, she'd been sleeping at all. He thrust the bag into the refrigerator, hoping the ancient coils would put out enough coolness to keep the beer and eggs cold, and then he went in search of Lizzie.

She was sitting in the middle of the front parlor. When he'd been growing up, most of his friends had had living rooms, family rooms, rec rooms, dens. His mother had had a parlor.

The furniture was old, valuable and miserably uncomfortable. Even beneath the film of dust Damien could see the highly polished wood floor, and antimacassars adorned each stiffly padded chair. Lizzie was standing in front of the huge fireplace that had never once held a fire, not even at Christmas, and her expression was far, far away.

"Want to clean?" he asked, goading her. As a matter of fact, he rather liked seeing his mother's spotless house in decline.

"No," she said, her voice distant. "You must be tired." She sounded no more than casually interested, and he remembered the way her voice had sounded just a few short hours ago, when she'd told him she was in love with him.

He wanted to hear that voice again. That passion. He wanted to bring her to life again, and him with it. She was too much like death already, with her pale face and her eerie stillness. As if she'd already given up, when he'd just begun to fight.

He wanted to cross the room, pull her into his arms and kiss her. He clenched his fists, forcing himself to stay put. "Yeah," he said. "While you were dreaming your way from Los Angeles to the desert, I was watching our tail."

"I wasn't asleep."

He believed her. "Then you must be tired, too. Where do you want to sleep?"

"Alone."

It shouldn't bother him, that flat, emotionless word. But it did. "I meant, did you want to sleep upstairs in one of the bedrooms, or down here on the sofa?"

"I don't care," she said, her voice lifeless.

He wanted to slap her. He wanted to do something to bring her back to vibrant, seething anger. The kind of anger he was feeling, right now, at the waste of another woman's fragile life. And for his own culpability. "Go find yourself a bed, then," he said, shuttering his own feelings. "I'll see what I can do to make this place habitable, at least for the next few days."

She managed a look of mild derision—a good sign, he thought. If she could summon forth that much feeling, there was hope for her. But then she turned and drifted away, like some damned ghost, and he heard the creaking of the stairs as she climbed upward.

He wanted to run to the bottom of the stairs, to call up to her and tell her not to use his mother's bedroom, but he kept still. It was a foolish thought on his part. His mother was long gone. Her repressed, depressive nature would no longer inhabit that gloomy room. It wouldn't reach out and catch Lizzie in its dark tendrils.

He glanced around him. The dust didn't trouble him, but the musty smell did. He wasn't sure if the hot, thick air of the Santa Ana winds was much of an improvement, but at least it lessened his claustrophobia and gave the old house something it had never experienced before. In the past, when the Santa Anas had blown, his mother had shut all the windows, pulled all the shades and sat alone in the suffocating darkness.

Water would be a nice option, too. He would have to prime the pump. That was something he hadn't done for more than fifteen years, but he imagined it was somewhat like riding a bicycle. Once you got the knack of it, you never forgot. Once he got the water heater up and running, the house aired out and enough firewood stacked to combat the chilly night air, then he, too, might consider taking a nap. Sleeping away the bright, useless hours of daylight. So that he'd be ready once more to do battle with the night.

The pump was more stubborn than he remembered, and it was well into the afternoon when he finally got the water pressure at a stable rate, a pile of very dry wood by the fireplace and a cold beer in his hand. He'd decided against tequila—he would need all his wits about him. There was nothing between Lizzie and certain, gruesome death but his own poor efforts, and he couldn't afford to have anything clouding those efforts. No matter how much he longed to just turn everything off.

The gloomy house had darkened in the afternoon, and the sky was growing dark, roiling with clouds. Damien didn't make the mistake of thinking there might be a storm. It seldom rained in the desert—and it certainly wasn't about to start now.

He would have thought the heat and sun would be a relief after what seemed like a decade of rain. Instead, the bright desert sun had been its own oppression, mocking the dark night of terror that life had become.

He was getting fanciful, he thought, climbing that long flight of stairs, the half-empty can of beer in his hand, automatically avoiding the fourth step that always creaked to inform his listening mother that he was sneaking in late. Lizzie would probably be lying in her dark room, in the middle of her big, dark bed. He didn't want her in there, but he would let her be. She needed whatever rest she could find.

He couldn't resist checking in on her. He peered inside the open door of his mother's bedroom at the top of the stairs. The maroon velvet curtains were drawn, the muddy brown quilt unwrinkled on top of the bed. The tarnished silver brush and mirror lay on the doily-covered dresser, untouched, next to the picture of a stiff, unhappy-looking couple. His parents had looked miserable even on their wedding day. If his father hadn't been killed in a car accident, he probably would have abandoned them.

He moved over to the curtains, pulling them, flooding the room with light, staring at the wasted remains of his mother's cold, unhappy life. He'd never been able to make up for the loss of his father and brother. She'd always found him wanting, always expected more than he was able to give, and finally he'd stopped trying, content simply to escape.

Until she'd died, alone, unhappy, just as she'd lived her life. And for the first time he felt no guilt.

She'd chosen her way, closing herself off from life, from her only surviving son. Shutting herself away when things grew too much for her. It had always been her choice, and she had paid for it with the empty years of her life.

And he had made the same choice. He'd become just like her during the past year, locked in a derelict apartment that wasn't that far removed from his mother's spotless mausoleum, in spirit if not in neatness. And the truth of that revelation scorched his soul.

He shook himself. It was past time to be hating her, past time to be hating himself. If he was going to keep Lizzie alive, then he was going to have to reenter life fully, not hide away, afraid of what he might find out. He was going to have to face life, face death.

And so was Lizzie.

She wasn't in his brother's room, that spotless, soulless little guest room that looked as if no one had ever grown up there, lived there. She wasn't in the sewing room, on that narrow cot where his mother had spent many a night when his father was still alive.

She was in his room. Lying in his narrow boy's bed, with the Princeton blanket thrown over her, her red hair spread out over the pillows that had once held his adolescent fantasies.

Her choice of rooms hadn't been accidental. His track trophies were on one shelf, his journalism awards on another. There was a poster of some California actress in a bikini, the object of his adolescent sexual fantasies, and James Dean glowering down from another wall, teenage angst personified. Damien looked around him and suddenly felt more alive than he had in years.

He was human. He'd made mistakes, horrible mistakes. But he would survive. He could even do what he could to right those wrongs. Starting with the woman lying asleep in his teenage bed. He'd spent hundreds of nights lying in that same bed, wishing he had a woman with him. Now, finally, his fantasies were being fulfilled. And not by just any woman. Not by the California blonde and her perfect, silicone-enhanced endowments. But by a real woman. One who'd somehow managed to get closer to him than he'd ever allowed anyone to get. One he'd somehow managed to care about.

He wasn't going to get on that bed with her. He would have given ten years off his life to do so, but he wouldn't give ten years off hers. And it could mean just that. His instincts told him that the Ripper was nowhere around—that they'd lost him for the time being. But how long that respite would last, or whether he could even trust his instincts, was anybody's guess.

He sank down on the floor, leaning against the wall, taking another long sip of his beer. He stretched his legs out in front of him, watching her as she slept, watching over her. At least, for now, she was safe. It was the most he could ask.

It was cold and dark when Lizzie awoke. She was lying huddled beneath a scratchy wool blanket, in what had to be Damien's bedroom, and for a moment she didn't move. She hated this house. Hated the dust and the gloom and the smell of wasted lives. Hated the antique furniture and the tiny-flowered wallpaper, all in muddy shades of brown. She hated the feeling of hopelessness that permeated the place. How in God's name had Damien survived such a gloomy upbringing?

He was with her, she knew it with an instinctive sense of comfort, though he hadn't joined her on the narrow bed. It was just as well. She had a thin casing of ice around her—if he touched her with his warm, deft hands, that ice would crack, and the pain would be too much to bear. She was better off this way. Safe, inviolate.

She sat up slowly, quietly. In the darkness she could see Damien leaning against the wall, sound asleep, his long dark hair fallen in his face. He didn't look much older than the boy who'd grown up in this room, and she wondered what he'd been like back then, when life was pure and clean and simple.

Except that life could never have been pure and clean and simple in a dark, haunted house like this one. It was no wonder he kept away, no wonder he called it his mother's house, never his own. If it were hers, she would repudiate it, as well, she who had never really had a home or a mother.

She slid out of bed, on the opposite side from him, and moved quietly out of the room. She didn't want to come close to him. He was too tempting, too heartbreaking. Besides, there was something she had to do, and she suspected he might try to stop her.

The house was bitterly cold, and it was a shock after the thick dry heat of the day. She'd never spent much time in the desert, and with good reason. She wanted mountains and sunlight and clean, fresh air. This place was almost as bad as the postindustrial drizzle of Los Angeles.

In the best of times, she was a practical woman. This was far from the best of times, but she was able to do what she had to with calm efficiency, her brain on automatic pilot, as she checked the damper, opened it. No birds or animals had made their nests in Mrs. Damien's cold, gloomy house. Even they had felt unwelcome.

Damien had done his part—the wood and kindling lay stacked next to the huge fireplace. She laid the fire with calm efficiency, using newspapers that were more than ten years old, and she watched the flames as if hypnotized.

Fires were supposed to be so comforting, so romantic. She felt the heat of the blaze, and it chilled her to her soul. She waited until the blaze had caught, biting into the old, dry logs, and then she reached for the first mask.

There were seventeen of them. She sat back on her knees and watched, dry-eyed, patient, as each one caught fire in turn, the papier-mâché igniting, the yarn and cloth sizzling and melting, the clay cracking, the jewels falling off into the coals, the faces dissolving. Seventeen of them, monsters and clowns, divas and grandes dames, children and grandparents and dragons and dogs. Seventeen masks that the Ripper would never use.

It wasn't until her hands reached for the final mask that some of her icy composure began to crack. The room was pitch-dark now, except for the macabre, dancing flames of the funeral pyre, but the heat barely penetrated the bitterly cold room. The last mask had been wrapped in an afghan and tissue paper, handled with loving care. She stared down at the childish Lizzie, and the pain began to seep back.

"Don't do it, Lizzie," he said. His voice was calm, low, soothing, and yet urgent. She hadn't heard him descend those stairs, hadn't known he'd been watching.

She didn't turn to look at him. Her face was wet now, and she wasn't sure if it was sweat from the chilly fire, or tears. She didn't want to know. "I have to. You know it as well as I do," she said, but her fingers tightened on the mask, unable to make the final move.

And then he was beside her, kneeling on the floor, and his hands were on the mask, as well, so that it lay between them. "Don't, Lizzie. We'll keep this one safe. We'll keep you safe. Don't burn it."

He tugged, and she let it go, watching as he set it back in the basket. And then he leaned over and put his mouth against hers in a kiss of such gentle passion that the ice around her heart began to shatter. She reached up to his shoulders, to cling to him, as she felt longing suffuse her, a need so powerful it went beyond passion, beyond sex, into a need for life itself, a need to taste, to know. Him, the man who called to her over the years, over the lifetimes. "I love you, Killian," she said. And then she pulled back, staring at him in utter horror, as she realized what name she'd called him.

Killian. The man from a century ago. The man who had let Mary Kelly and Lizzie Stride die. The man she'd loved so many years before. And she'd known it was him.

CHAPTER FOURTEEN

Damien surged to his feet, reaching down and hauling her up with him, and there was no gentleness in his touch. "You're getting out of here," he said roughly.

"What are you talking about?" She tried to pull away, to pull her cocoon back around her, but the noise and confusion were battering her, and she couldn't hide.

"You're not safe with me. I'm taking you to Adamson. I can make him put you under protective custody. I can get a headline in the *Chronicle* so fast it'll make the Rodney King case look like a simple mistake. He'll take care of you...."

"No!" She jerked out of his grip. "I don't trust him. I don't trust anyone. No one can keep me safe, not if the Ripper's determined to get me. The only one I stand a chance with is you."

"Don't you understand, Lizzie? I'm afraid of what might happen to you if I'm the one. Women have died because of me so many times. So damned many times. I can't let you be one of them."

"Damien ..."

"Don't you see it happening to you? You're shutting off, just like I did, just like my mother did. You'll sit in this house and wait for death, and I'll be off somewhere, trying to stop him and failing. Either that, or I'll be here, and I'll *be* him."

"You're not the Ripper!" she cried, the sound torn
out of her, shattering the last of her defenses. She
reached up and caught his shoulders, wanting to shake
some sense into him, but he was too big, too strong.
"Don't you think I'd know?"

"Lizzie," he said wearily, "all those women trusted
him. All those women thought they knew, too. They
thought they were safe, and they weren't. No one's safe.
I'm taking you out of here." He caught her wrist, but
she slid around, inside his arms, coming up tight against
him, and all her apathy had vanished, leaving fury,
panic and determination.

"You're not taking me anywhere," she said, putting
her arms around his waist, holding him. And then she
reached up, caught his face with her hands and kissed
him, her mouth open against his.

He tried to fight it; she could feel the tension in his
body as he fought both his own need and hers. But she
was inexorable, despite her fear. She held him tightly
against her body, kissing his unresponsive mouth, and
then, suddenly, he came alive, slanting his lips across
hers, using his tongue far more effectively than she
could as he pulled her into his arms, her hips tight
against his so that she could feel the heat of his wanting.

She slid her hands between their bodies, found his
shirt and ripped it open. His own hands were already
under her loose T-shirt, cupping her breasts as they
hardened against his fingers. And then he pulled the
shirt over her head, sending it sailing across the room,
and his mouth was on her breast, hot, suckling, sending shivers of desire down into her belly, and she made
a soft, quiet whimper of desire.

"Don't stop," she whispered against his hair. "If you stop this time, I'll kill you."

His only answer was to reach for the waistband of her jeans, unfastening them with one rough movement and pushing them down her hips, her plain white panties with them. She kicked out of them, standing there in the firelight, naked, waiting for him, looking into his dark, tormented face unflinchingly, as she reached out and put her hand against his zipper, pressing, hard, as he stared down at her, panting, distant.

He tried to pull back as one last vestige of sanity penetrated his need. "I'll hurt you," he said in a hoarse voice. "I don't want to...."

"Yes, you do," she said, sinking to her knees in front of him, pressing her face against the front of his jeans, feeling the heat and desire pulsing through him. "Hurt me if you have to. I need you, and you need me. You need to go to the edge, to know you'll come back."

"What if I don't?" His fingers threaded through her hair, but he wasn't pulling away. "What if I don't come back?"

She turned and kissed him through the metal zipper and the layers of denim, and she felt him pulse against her mouth. "I'll take that risk." And she reached up and unsnapped his jeans with trembling hands.

A shudder washed over him, and she knew he'd given up his control, released the last remnants of sanity. It was too late to change her mind, to pull back, and she quashed her temporary throb of fear. She'd come this far—she wasn't going to let either of them call a halt to it until they faced their demons.

He hauled her up into his arms, roughly, wrapping her legs around his waist. He looked dark, remote, not the man she thought she knew, as he shoved her up against the wall, one hand fumbling with his jeans, freeing himself.

He pushed into her, hard, filling her, and she braced herself, welcoming him, no longer worrying about pain, only needing him, more of him, all of him. Her face was crushed against his shoulder as she felt him thrust into her, and she cradled his head, holding on, wanting nothing but his release, his pleasure to fill her.

It was darkness, madness, blood and death. With each thrust of his body she went a little farther, a little deeper, lost in some world where nothing remained but the inexplicable, powerful feelings surging through her body, the sound of his breathing in her ear, the beating of his heart against hers, the slick sweat on his skin as he surged into her, again and again and again, deep and hard and eternal.

He went rigid in her arms, and she clutched him tightly, desperate, afraid he might leave her. He made a sound, a harsh, lonesome cry of pain and completion, as he filled her with his desire. And then she shattered around him, torn away from everything she'd known, and there was just their joining, pulsing, wet, complete.

He leaned his forehead against the wall, beside her head, and then he slammed it, hard, against the surface. He pulled free from her body, lowering her, but her knees were too shaky to hold her, and he had no choice but to put his arms around her. "Damn," he said. He sat on the floor, cradling her in his lap, the firelight sending stark patterns across their sweat-damp skin. "Damn," he said again, this time a little softer, a little more wondering.

Lizzie looked up at him, uncertain, shy. She reached up and brushed a thick lock of black hair away from his face. "Why *damn?* We made love and survived. I'm still in one piece," she said. She glanced down at her body, sprawled across his. "I think."

She managed to coax the faintest glimmer of a smile. "Just damn, Lizzie," he murmured, but his hands were gentle on her, wrapping her tight against him. "Just damn."

He knew where they were. It had taken him hours, endless, damnable hours, but he had finally traced them. Damien had inherited a house in a small town in the California desert. A simple phone call verified that the place hadn't been inhabited for years, that someone answering Damien's description had gone into one of the new convenience stores that were springing up in all the outlying towns as civilization crept in. He knew where they were, and he knew how to find them.

He was in a hurry. His time was running out; he knew that. Twenty-four hours was all he had now, and he had to use it wisely.

He'd used the last mask on the old man. He hadn't wanted to, but when he'd stared into those sightless eyes he'd known Hickory had wanted the mask, and he'd put it over his face, shutting out that dead stare.

He would have to find a new one. One more. The stores were empty; he'd ascertained that days ago. He could try to track down private collectors, but that would take too long, even with his resources.

No, he knew where he would find the mask he needed. With the person whose destiny it was to wear it. He would find it with Long Liz Stride. And this time he would finish the job, good and proper.

It would take four hours to drive out to Damien's house. He could take his time. Stop for a cup of coffee and some soggy doughnuts. Maybe even take a dozen home, for later.

Because later his work would be done. For this life-time. He could go back to his usual business and forget all about the past three months. He would have done what he had to. It would be over.

Damien watched her as she slept. There was a curi-ous kind of peace in it, knowing that at least for now he had kept her safe. She looked exhausted. He could see the pale mauve shadows beneath her closed eyes. He could see the faint swelling of her mouth, bruised by his kisses. He'd marked her. And he still wanted her.

Still in one piece, she'd said, although she hadn't sounded quite sure of it. She'd stumbled when he sent her to take a long, soaking bath, and when she'd emerged, pink-limbed, fresh-faced and shy, he'd al-most ripped off the oversize T-shirt he'd unearthed from his drawers upstairs.

He'd brought down one of the mattresses and set it on the floor in front of the fire. She'd looked at it, managed a sleepy smile that was almost as erotic as her long pink legs, and said, "No sheets?" But she'd lain down on it anyway, drifting effortlessly into sleep as he watched her.

He'd waited until she was soundly asleep before he took his own shower, then came back and fed the fire, placing fresh logs on the coals that held the remnants of her masks.

He wanted to stretch out on the mattress with her, draw her into his arms and hold her. He wanted to make love to her. They'd had sex, hot, hard, quick sex, and he hadn't turned into a monster. Now he wanted to make slow, languorous love to her, to taste every inch of her body, to kiss her into a daze of pleasure.

He still didn't trust himself. Didn't trust the creatures of the night, the creature who hunted them both. Somewhere out there, Jack the Ripper was waiting. No longer did Damien fear that the Ripper hid inside his own twisted heart. He wasn't the Ripper.

But he shared his own piece of culpability. And if he wasn't careful, that responsibility would spread into this lifetime, into the woman who lay sleeping so soundly, so trustingly.

It was foggy that night. But then, there was nothing unusual about that—London in the autumn was usually plagued with fog, and 1888 had had more than its fair share. She didn't mind. It made for a bit of privacy, and she was always one for privacy. Growing up in a one-room shanty with twelve brothers and sisters, your own parents rutting away close by, made you long for a bit of peace.

At least she was as far away from Ireland as her money could take her. And London had been good to Mary Kelly. She was a pretty girl, prettier than most, and she got more customers than most. Nicer ones, gentlemen, mostly. Ones with soft hands and kind words, who just liked a bit of sport now and then, something different from what their wives would offer them. And Mary Kelly was willing, for a price.

She didn't like men much. They were usually bullies, like her father and brothers, intent on either beating or bedding a woman, and it didn't matter if she was your own kin or not. She'd put up with it because she was too small, too weak, to fight, and then she'd left. And the men who came down to Spitalfields in search of a bit of female companionship were at least a sight better than her own brothers.

She had no intention of being in the business for long. Just until she got together enough money to get her to France. She wasn't going to be a whore in France, mind you. She would arrive in Paris with enough money to keep her going, long enough to find a rich man who would fancy a pretty girl of his own. One who might put forward the cash to start her on a career on the stage. Mary Kelly could sing, she could dance, and she could recite in a loud, clear voice. By the time she returned to London she would take the city by storm. Mrs. Langtry would pale in comparison.

There were only two things in the way of this stellar plan. Jack the Ripper. And James Killian.

The Ripper didn't frighten her. She was a clever one, not the sort to go off with a stranger, no matter how much money he dangled in front of her. The women he'd killed had been old, in their forties, toothless, worn-out old crones who would lift their skirts for a bob and then be on their way. Even poor Lizzie Stride had usually been too drunk to notice who she went with, as long as they gave her enough for her night's lodging and a bag of cashews.

Lizzie. They'd been good friends, despite the difference in their ages. Not like Cathy Eddowes, the old bitch. It was Lizzie's death that had made the difference. It was Lizzie's death that pushed Mary Kelly into talking to that nosey reporter.

He was nice enough looking, she supposed. His suit was a little too flashy. She had good taste, Mary did, and knew what a real gentleman should be wearing. That diamond on his left hand was a sizable one, and at first she thought she might be able to talk him into parting with it. It would have gone a good ways toward her passage to France.

But Jack Killian was a downy one, and he knew what he wanted. Told her flat out that he'd never had to pay for it and never would. She could keep her skirts down and her eyes up—he wasn't interested.

She'd known it was a lie. The way his brown eyes lingered over her breasts, the way his hand reached out for her, then dropped before he could touch her. He wanted her, all right. And the surprising thing was, she wanted him. For the first time in her life, she actually wanted a man.

He had a plan, he said, drawing her to a private table at the Ten Bells Pub and plying her with hot shandies. She watched what she drank—she needed her wits about her or she would end up like Cathy or Lizzie. But Killian's plan was a good one, a chance worth taking. If the two of them could trap the Ripper, then she could write her own ticket. She wouldn't need to go to Paris to go on the stage. She would be deluged by offers right here in London. They would call her the heroine of Whitechapel, Killian told her, his voice soft and persuasive. People would flock to see her.

Tomorrow night, he told her. He'd already bought a gun, and tomorrow night they would lay their trap. The Ripper wanted her, Jack said, though he never told her how he knew. The two of them would lure him back to her room, and then, quick as you could say "Bob's your uncle," Killian would burst in with the gun. He would kill him, if he had to, and his own career would be made as well.

Mary looked at him across the table, at the handsome mouth beneath the handlebar mustache, the determined brown eyes. "You've got it all figgered, haven't you?"

"It can't fail," he said flatly. "You trust me, don't you, Mary? I wouldn't let anything happen to you."

"I've never trusted a man in me life," she said pertly, tossing her head back and staring at him.

His gaze dropped to her mouth, and she knew what he was thinking. And for the first time in her life, an answering warmth filled her. "You can trust me," he said. "I've got as much to gain as you do."

"Not as much to lose, however," she pointed out.

He just stared at her for a moment. "I wouldn't want to lose you," he said, the words soft and unexpected.

She didn't move. "I thought you weren't interested."

"I said I wasn't going to buy it. I don't want ten minutes beneath your skirts, Mary. I don't want a couple of nights, either. I want everything." He looked at her, and the dark longing was stark in his eyes, reaching into her heart and squeezing. "I want forever."

He kissed her then. She hadn't been kissed in years. Most of her customers weren't interested in preliminaries, and she found it kept things more impersonal. But he leaned across the table and brushed his lips against hers, and something inside her blossomed into life.

Her lips clung to his for a brief, eternal moment, and then she leaned back, feeling the unexpected sting of tears in her eyes. She never kissed, and she never cried. "Killian…" she said, wanting to tell him she loved him, but he stopped her.

"I know, Mary," he said wryly. "You want a rich man and a comfortable life. I can't compete with the kind of thing you're looking for."

"If we catch the Ripper you'll be famous," she said. "If you're famous, you'll be rich."

His eyes met hers. "Yes."

"Tomorrow night," she said, suddenly brisk.

He didn't move. Then he shook his head. "I've changed my mind. It's too dangerous."

"Don't be daft, man," she said, feeling suddenly, gloriously happy and completely invulnerable. "You'll be watching and I wasn't born yesterday. I'm not like those poor old hags. I'll be on my guard. We'll do it, Killian. We'll catch the Ripper. And we'll live happily ever after. Together."

She rose, leaning down to kiss him again, and his hand reached up and touched her breast. She wanted to press against his hand, to know the pleasure he could give her, pleasure that no man ever had ever given her, but she had work to do. She pulled away regretfully, smiling at him.

"Where are you going?"

"I've got to meet someone."

"Don't, Mary," he said. "It's too dangerous."

"Lord love you, I'm not going to turn any tricks tonight," she said cheerfully. "After I've promised you my hand and heart? Not to mention the rest of me. I've got to go pay me rent, or I'll be out on the streets come morning, and then what will we do? Cheer up, Killian. We'll be fine."

She paused in the door, waggling her fingers at him, and he stared after her. And it wasn't until she stepped out into the fog-shrouded darkness that she wondered whether he believed her story for even one moment.

He might come after her. And she didn't have much time to lose. She intended to give up the life—indeed, the thought of meeting her customer tonight gave her the cold chills. Not that he was a bad sort, mind you. And he was just the kind of man who could do a girl a good turn when she needed it.

Besides, he was very generous. She would take the last ten quid and stash it with the rest of her savings, and Killian need never know that she'd turned one last trick.

She was humming under her breath, something Irish and lively. She was going to like what James Killian did to her body. It was going to be different from all the other men, hunching over her, sweating and panting and heaving.

She heard the knock at the door as she was stripping off her half-gloves. Some of the other girls were nervous, but not Mary Kelly. Not with tonight's customer. He was one of her regulars—this would be his fourth time in the past few months. He'd come to her each night the Ripper struck, poor man, and she could understand his need for a little bit of forgetfulness.

She opened the door and saw him, his face bland and kind and familiar. He was carrying a bag this time, but she paid it scant heed, opening the door and ushering him in before anyone could see him. "Hello, Chief Inspector," she said brightly, reaching for the buttons on the front of her dress.

"Hello, Mary," he said, setting the case down on the foot of the bed. "I've got a surprise for you."

She smiled brightly, ignoring her inward sigh of boredom. "Oh, I love surprises," she said.

The chief inspector in charge of the Ripper case chuckled. "You'll love this one, lass."

Killian raced down the alleyways, his fancy new shoes skidding on the wet cobblestones. She'd lied to him, he knew it, and he'd let her do it. He had the gun in his pocket—if the Ripper was coming after her tonight, he would be the one to stop him.

He had considered for a moment, for a brief moment, that he would call it all off. Forget the Ripper, take Mary Kelly home with him, off the streets and keep her safe. But it had been no choice at all. They were too ambitious, the both of them. He didn't want a scratch-penny existence with a drab of a wife. He wanted everything, fame and fortune and Mary by his side. It was a risk worth taking. And he was going to let her take that risk.

She would be in her room by now, and he would sit outside and wait, wait until her client showed up. He would be fast enough to stop him, and then he would give the girl such a backhand across her pretty little face that she would never consider lying to him again. And then he would kiss her. And Springheeled Jack would just have to look on and suffer.

There was a light on in her room when he reached the alleyway, but no sound came from within. She was still alone, then, waiting for her customer. James Killian pushed himself back into a corner, waiting. If it was someone he knew, he would just scare him away. If it was a stranger, he would wait and listen, the gun at the ready. By tomorrow morning, their future, his and Mary's, would be bright.

He must have dozed off. When he awoke, it was morning, and his body felt damp, stiff and cramped. There was no light on in Mary's room, and he cursed himself for distrusting her. He wanted to touch her, to kiss her. He crossed the empty alleyway and reached for her door, planning to knock and wake her up.

It wasn't shut entirely. It opened at the slightest pressure, opened wide. Jack Killian stood in the doorway, staring into the interior of the room, and began to scream.

She was there. Lizzie, Mary, whoever she was, was there, her arms wrapped around him, her hands shaking, and she was holding him, kissing him. She was alive, and so was he, and the grisly nightmare was over. Damien pushed her down on the mattress and she went willingly, and in her mouth was the sweetness he'd tasted, more than a hundred years before, when he'd first kissed Mary Kelly at the Ten Bells.

CHAPTER FIFTEEN

Lizzie wrapped her arms around him, her body softening beneath his as he covered her. The sound of his scream had torn her from her dream, and for a moment she'd been lost, disoriented. It had felt so real.

But there was no reality now but the horsehair mattress beneath her back, the flickering firelight as it danced across her skin, the feel of his body against hers, hard and hot in the darkened room.

His face looked almost brutal in the firelight, but she didn't believe in that brutality. She cupped his face with her hands and kissed him slowly, fully, prepared for the onslaught of his demon-driven desire.

It didn't come. There was no anger, no hurry, just warm, sweet arousal that curled slowly through her body and his as he kissed her back, tasting her, settling his body against hers so that she was in no doubt about how much he wanted her, and in no doubt that they were going to take their time.

He kissed her mouth, her cheekbones, her sensitive ears. His hands slid down between their bodies, covering her breasts through the soft, worn material of the oversize T-shirt, but his touch was gentle, caressing and almost unbearably arousing. She whimpered with a wordless longing, but his mouth simply covered hers, drinking in her soft protest, as his hands moved lower, between her legs, touching her.

Suddenly she was afraid. Not of his violence—she'd surrendered to that and survived, gloriously intact. She was afraid of his tenderness. Afraid of his love.

She tried to move away, but he stopped her by the simple expedient of placing his body over hers again, holding her still with the solid, inexorable weight of him.

"What are you afraid of, Lizzie?"

She forced herself to look up at him, into eyes that were dark, but not brown, into a face that was long and narrow and faintly stubbled with beard, not square and adorned with side-whiskers and a flowing mustache. She looked up at him and saw another man, one she'd loved long, long ago.

"It's been so long," she blurted, knowing how foolish it would sound to a man who'd made love to her only a few hours ago, but saying it anyway.

But he didn't even smile. "Too long," he said. "A century." And then he kissed her slowly, his gentleness sliding into a shimmering sensuality that left her hot and damp and panting for breath.

He pulled back, resting on his knees, watching her as he began to unfasten his jeans. She lay there, watching for a moment, and then she reached up, covering his hand, stopping him. "Let me," she whispered, unfastening the zipper, freeing him, pushing the rest of his clothes off him with a deftness she had never known she possessed.

His body was lean and wiry and golden in the firelight, a runner's body. She slid her hands up his chest, placing her mouth against his neck as she pushed him down on the mattress. He tasted of soap, of skin, of something dark and wonderful. She moved her mouth downward, over his flat belly, kissing, biting, tasting.

And then she took him in her mouth, the full, silky length of him, consuming him, consumed by him, lost in an act she had never performed, not in this lifetime, and never with love.

His hands caught her shoulders, his long fingers caressing, and she could hear the strangled sound of his breathing, taste the salty sweetness of his desire, feel the blood course through his body. The night closed down around them, and there was nothing to fear, only the two of them, and she wanted this, she wanted him.

She felt his hands tighten on her as he pulled her away, and she let out a cry of protest, of frustration, but it was too late. He pushed her down on the mattress, kneeling between her legs, and he was huge and shadowy and everything she had ever wanted.

She spread her legs for him, closing her eyes as his hands cupped her hips, and waited for the thrust that would fill her.

A moment later, her eyes shot open when he set his mouth between her legs, using his tongue, his teeth, his lips, to bring her to the precipice, and she knew her first fear. And then there was no room for fear and she leapt over the edge, her body dissolving into an endless convulsion that stole her breath, her heartbeat, her mind and soul.

He waited, watching her, as she struggled to return to reality. He waited long enough for her to catch her breath, for her eyes to focus, and then he moved, sheathing himself inside her with one strong, liquid thrust, setting his mouth against hers.

She felt taken, possessed, lost. She felt triumphant, possessive, found. She raised her hips, bracing herself against the mattress to meet him, and she kissed him back.

The rhythm of their bodies was slow and easy as they rocked back and forth on the old mattress. She could feel the tension build once more, and she reached for it, like a greedy child, but Damien moved, forestalling her, slowing it down, only to build it ever more strongly.

He rolled over on his back, taking her with him, looking up at her as she moved over his body, the two of them slick with sweat as the firelight cast eerie shadows across their skin. He reached out and caught her hips, but let her set the pace, his face drawn taut with the effort of control.

She felt smooth, sleek and powerful. "Don't fight it," she whispered in the darkness. "Give yourself to me. Now, Damien."

His eyes shut tight. "Now," he said. "Now." And he thrust up into her, hard, filling her with his warmth, his wetness, his love.

She took it, all of it, her body drinking it in, taking him, owning him, reveling in the moment, her own body clenching tightly, lost and found, as she claimed him. She collapsed on top of him, a weary, panting little mass of humanity, and she could feel the stray shudders racking his body as his strong arms came around her, holding her, cradling her against him.

She wanted to say something. To tell him that she loved him, no matter what he did, that she had always loved him, throughout time. It had been her fault, opening the door to the man she thought she could trust, so certain she was safe when he'd warned her she wasn't. He'd blamed himself for decades upon decades, and she had to tell him it was all right, that they had another chance.

But there were no words. He rolled onto his side, tucking her tightly against him, and her face hid against his shoulder, naturally, comfortably, shutting out the night and the demons that would gather once more. The bright fire of their love could only penetrate a small way into the blackness. And then the night took over once more.

She could feel his hand soothing her hair away from her face, feel the soft touch of his lips against her temple. Hear the murmur of words, gentle, meaningless words, of love, of commitment, of happily-ever-afters that they might never see.

She heard it all, her body warming and softening against him as she fought with her memory. She'd seen something. In her dream, she'd seen the kindly, familiar face of the man who had killed her. The answer was there, but she was too weary, too sated, to reach for it.

Instead, she sighed, giving up the last of her control, giving everything to Damien, melting against him. And the last thing she heard before she drifted off to sleep was the sound of her name on his lips. "Mary," he said, and his voice came from far away, from across decades. "I love you forever."

Lizzie awoke slowly, by degrees, accepting her surroundings with a surprising calm. Light was filtering through the closed shades, the bright, merciless light of the desert, and the house fell hot, stale and musty. There were still coals in the fireplace directly in front of her eyes, but she'd kicked off whatever covers she'd used during the night. She was lying on the mattress, stark naked. And utterly alone.

She found her discarded T-shirt, pulled it on and rose on unsteady feet. It had been a long night, and she felt damp, sticky and slightly sore. She hugged herself tightly for a moment, wishing it were Damien's arms and not her own. And then she went in search of him.

There was no sign of him upstairs. She headed into the bathroom, washed quickly and pulled on her discarded clothes. By the time she reached the kitchen, she was feeling somewhat more human, lured by the smell of coffee and the certainty that she would see Damien.

There was coffee, all right. But sitting at the table, a doleful expression on his face, was Detective Finlay Adamson.

Lizzie almost screamed, swallowing her instinctive panic before she could give in to it. "You scared me," she said, reaching for the coffeepot, casting a surreptitious glance around the room for a trace of Damien.

"I'm sorry," he said. "I just got here, and I heard the shower going. I didn't want to walk in on you."

"How did you find us?"

"County records."

"Damien said this place wasn't in his name."

"He pays taxes on it just the same," Adamson said. "It took a while, but I was able to trace it. Where is he?"

She took a deep, meditative sip of the coffee. It was absolutely horrible—Damien must have made it. "What do you mean?"

"There's no sign of him, and the car's gone. Where did he go?"

I won't panic, she told herself, sinking down in the hard wooden chair opposite Adamson. There's a logical explanation for all this, I know there is.

Her eyes met his. "I don't know," she said simply.

Adamson took a deep breath, and she could feel the concern running through him. "Lizzie," he said, "I don't know how to tell you this."

"Tell me what?"

"I think you should get away from here. Away from Damien. He probably heard me coming, and he's just waiting until I leave. And then it will be too late for you, Lizzie. He'll kill you, as he killed all the others."

"Don't be ridiculous!" She jumped up, knocking her coffee over. "Damien isn't the Ripper! I've been with him during the most recent killings, been right by his side. He couldn't—"

"Don't trust him, Lizzie. You haven't been awake, watching him. You've been sleeping. I expect you might even have been drugged. The Ripper works fast—it doesn't take that long to gut a body, if you've had a bit of practice."

"Don't," she said faintly, holding up a hand in protest.

"I'm trying to save your life. He murdered your friend, then let you find her. We have proof, Lizzie. Fingerprints. Witnesses. Physical evidence. We've been watching him for a long time, and we finally have enough to nail him. He's the Ripper, and he may not even know it. He's killed a dozen women, and you'll be the next one. He's even started to kill men."

She raised her eyes, staring at him. "Men?"

"An old man was found in your apartment, Lizzie." He tossed the newspaper onto the table, and the headline screamed at her. It wasn't the *Chronicle,* with its sense of discretion. It was one of the bloodier papers, and Hickory's dead face, streaked with blood, stared back at her in bright color. "He killed him, and he's going to kill you."

She should be feeling numb by now, Lizzie told herself. She shouldn't be able to hurt anymore. "He didn't have a chance to kill Hickory," she said, in one last, desperate attempt to deny it.

"You didn't leave him alone with him? Are you absolutely positive? Even for a moment?"

She remembered running out to the car, waiting there for Damien to join her. It had only been a matter of a minute or two. Hadn't it?

"Why would he kill Hickory?"

"Why would he do any of this? He's not sane, Lizzie. He's going to kill you next, if you don't get the hell out of here. He didn't... mutilate Hickory. He just cut his throat, and then left. It wouldn't have taken more than thirty seconds. But it took Hickory time to die. Long enough for him to write the name of the murderer in his own blood on your floor."

"I don't believe it."

"Are you willing to stake your life on it?" He reached out a hand and placed it on hers, comforting. "Let me take you back to Los Angeles, Lizzie. I can get you protective custody—they won't dare say no after the recent killings. It's your only hope until we catch that monster."

Lizzie pulled her hand away. "I'll wait for him," she said.

"Haven't you been listening to me? We have proof. He's the Ripper. Maybe not in every case—we still haven't ruled out the possibility of copycat killers. But there's no doubt at all that he killed Courtland Massey and at least five of the others."

"I'll wait for him," she said again.

Adamson shook his head. "You're as crazy as he is. At least there are no more masks, as far as we can tell. He used the last one on Hickory Potter."

"And he can't kill without a mask," Lizzie said dully. She turned and headed into the living room, moving to the basket at a run. The final mask, the mask Damien had told her to save, was gone.

It would be her death mask, she knew it. She knelt on the floor by the empty basket, and pain racked her body, so sharp that she wanted to cry out. Here was proof she couldn't hide from. She raised her eyes to meet Adamson's compassionate ones as he stood in the doorway.

"He'll kill you, Lizzie," he said. "Don't let him do it. If not for your sake, for his. You're in love with him, aren't you? In love with a man who wants to kill you. Who wants to cut your body into pieces and—"

"Stop it." It should have been a scream, but it was nothing more than a soundless whisper.

But Adamson heard. "Come with me, Lizzie. Only I can keep you safe from the Ripper."

She wouldn't cry. It was too mundane, too worthless a reaction to something that was unbearable, unacceptable and unbelievable.

But there was no other explanation. "I've heard that before," she said, her voice flat and expressionless. And she rose, letting Adamson take her hand and lead her out into the mercilessly bright desert sun.

"Haven't seen you around these parts in a long time, Johnny," the old woman behind the counter murmured.

He peered at her, finally putting a name to that withered old face. "Mrs. Ramirez," he said. "It's good to see you." It was a lie. Mrs. Ramirez was the nosiest woman in three counties, and she'd never tempered her gossip with the slightest bit of compassion. Not that he needed compassion, he thought. But his mother could have done with a bit. He pushed his basket across the small counter, and the old woman picked out the quart of milk, the cigarettes and the beer with the air of an archaeologist discovering stray treasures.

"When did you start smoking, Johnny?" she asked.

None of your damned business, he thought, but he managed to keep a relatively pleasant expression on his face. He needed to get back to the house. He hadn't wanted to leave Lizzie, even for a few minutes, but he'd needed to make a phone call, and his mother had never even owned a phone.

Things had begun falling together. The unbelievable suddenly seemed not just a remote possibility but the inescapable truth. And the only way he could do something about it was to call Adamson and ask him, outright.

But Adamson, as usual, had been nowhere to be found. And the fear had begun.

He'd refused to give in to it. He'd come to the small convenience store at the crossroads to make his phone call and to pick up a few necessities. If he panicked, it would give the powers of darkness a foothold.

"Got a girl, have you?" Mrs. Ramirez said, peering at the box of condoms he'd thrown in there before he realized who was working here.

"No," he said flatly, controlling his urgency. "A woman."

"They all liked you back then," she said. "Even my own daughter couldn't keep her eyes off you. You remember Stella? She was in the class behind you."

"Of course," he said, not remembering Stella at all.

"She's married now, with four kids. Drive her crazy, they do. She'll be excited to hear you were back in town.

Broke all the young girls' hearts back then. A regular lady-killer.'' She pushed his change across the counter.

He stared at her for a moment, and a sudden, life-affirming certainty filled him. He'd known, deep in his heart, from the moment he'd touched Lizzie. He knew now in his mind and soul, as well. "No," he said. "I'm not." And he grabbed his groceries and headed out the door.

A sense of doom was creeping up on him, growing stronger and stronger as he neared the old house. He shoved his foot to the floor, making the old Austin-Healey jerk forward, speeding along the deserted road. He skidded to a stop behind the old Victorian house, racing up the back steps without bothering to slam the car door, calling her name, telling himself that his fear was crazy, but panicking anyway.

"Lizzie," he yelled, slamming into the kitchen, hearing only his own voice echo back. "Lizzie!" he called again.

And then he saw the two coffee cups on the dusty wooden table.

"No," he moaned. It was a sound of deep pain. He stumbled forward into the living room, half expecting to see her lying on the mattress, sightless eyes staring upward. There was no sign of her.

He dived toward the basket, but the mask was gone, as well. With any luck, she'd taken it with her, keeping it from the killer. But who in God's name had she gone with? Who would she trust, more than him?

The answer was inescapable, and horrifying in its ramifications. She'd gone with the one man she thought represented authority and safety, just as Mary Kelly had been fool enough to go with the one man she thought was safe. The man who was never around when there was a killing, the man who had access to all knowledge.

She'd gone with Chief Detective Finlay Adamson. The Venice Ripper.

Adamson hadn't come after her in a police car, and that, at least, was something Lizzie could be grateful for. She'd ridden in his squad car too many times. This one was larger, and it didn't smell of sweat and cigarettes and urine. It smelled like leather and luxury, and the seats were comfortable. She leaned her head back, closing her eyes, unwilling to watch the landscape as they made their way back to Los Angeles and safety. She wanted to shut out everything.

"Penny for your thoughts," Adamson murmured, and she didn't bother to open her eyes.

"They're not pleasant."

"I didn't imagine they would be. Why did you run away with Damien? I tried to warn you...."

She shook her head, negating that line of questioning. "I still can't believe it."

"Believe it," he said. "Would a dying man write an innocent man's name in blood?"

She turned then, to look at him. "I don't know."

"If there's any other answer, we'll find it. We have to bring him in first. We've got an all-points bulletin out covering the southern half of the state. We'll pick him up, never you fear. He can't have gone far."

"Shouldn't you be doing something? Not wasting your time with me?"

Adamson turned his gaze straight ahead again, but his big hands clenched the steering wheel, then relaxed. "I should," he admitted reluctantly. "I was worried about you. Too many women have died on my watch, and I couldn't stand the thought of one more. I ought to be out there, coordinating the manhunt."

"You can drop me off someplace. . . ."

"It wouldn't be safe," he said.

"Listen, I imagine there are any number of places between here and Los Angeles where I can hide. Drop me off, and only you will know where I am."

He appeared to consider it. "You're safe until night-fall," he said slowly. "The Ripper can't kill in the daylight."

"How do you know that?"

Adamson shrugged. "Just a guess, really. No one's been killed in the daytime, with the exception of Courtland Massey, and according to the coroner's preliminary estimate she died just after dawn. The killer probably didn't even realize it was daybreak with all the rain and darkness around southern California. So far that's been his only mistake, and I don't think he'll make it again. Even the woman in West Covina was killed just after sunset. There's no way anyone will hurt you for another—" he glanced at his watch "—six hours. I could drop you off at a place I know, then come back and get you. You'd be safe there."

"Where?"

"I passed an old train station on the way in. It's been deserted for years, it's way out in the middle of nowhere, but it's still pretty sound. You could hide out there until I came back for you."

The idea should have terrified her. It didn't. "That sounds like a good idea," she said, unnaturally calm. She wanted to get away from Adamson, away from everyone, while she sorted through the unacceptable. That the hands that had touched her, made love to her, were stained with blood.

She would have thought the landscape would have changed as they headed west, but it seemed to grow scrubbier, more desertlike as he drove.

They turned off onto a secondary road following an overgrown set of railway tracks. The road ended at a deserted train station, one that probably hadn't seen passengers in more than fifty years.

"You drove by here earlier?"

"Took the wrong turn," he said easily. "It's unlocked."

"How do you know?"

"I was looking for a phone. Go on in. We're more than an hour from his house—there's no way Damien can find you. He's just a man, you know. Not some creature with supernatural powers. Just an ordinary man."

Lizzie closed her eyes for a moment, remembering. "Just an ordinary man," she echoed flatly.

"Go inside and keep low. Here." He reached into the back seat and handed her a satchel. "There's some food and water in there, and a blanket. If I'm late getting back, it might get cold. But don't come out for anyone else. If anyone comes, you hide. Don't answer them. Don't answer anyone but me. I'll be back after dark. You hear?"

"I hear."

"You promise? I'm trying to save your life, Lizzie. I won't let that mad dog get you."

She forced herself to summon an ounce of gratitude she couldn't feel, and she reached out and touched his arm. He jerked away, as if burned, but his smile was warm and concerned.

"Thank you, Mr. Adamson. I promise." And she slid out of the big car and made her way into the deserted train station.

CHAPTER SIXTEEN

His hands shook with excitement and disgust as he drove away from the train station. Damien had taken her in carnal lust. She smelled of him. There was no longer any reason to delay. He had her, safely stashed away where no one would ever find her. He had the mask tucked safely in the trunk of his rental car, and he had his knife and his plastic raincoat to keep his clothes clean. All he had to do was wait until sundown.

He giggled softly as he drove along the deserted highway. It would finally be over, more than a hundred years after he'd started. He would finally finish what he was supposed to do. Lizzie Stride would share in the fate of her sisters.

And then he could rest.

It would be a fitting finale. Tonight it would be no bag lady, no teenage boy, none of the many personas that had confused the people who watched. Tonight he would use the final mask. And then he would place it over her face, when he was finished with her, and he would be gone.

He wondered briefly what would happen to Damien. He'd been cleared as a suspect weeks ago, and there had been nothing new that could link him to the killings, despite Adamson's best efforts. He would simply live out the rest of his life, racked with guilt because he hadn't been able to save Lizzie Stride. Adamson gave him no more than a couple of years before he wrapped that sports car around a tree.

And this would all be a dream. Once he finished tonight, the darkness would leave him. His destiny would be fulfilled, and he could continue with his life's work. Keeping the streets of Venice, California, safe from muggers and hookers and parasites. And no one would ever know of the darkness that had lived in him one autumn.

He was tired. He'd worked hard and long, getting to this point. One more day to live through, and then he would take his reward. He only wished he could make Damien watch.

Damien had no gun. Nothing to fight the Ripper with, nothing to stop him. He didn't waste his time heading back for the crossroads store and the pay telephone. No one would believe him. Finlay Adamson was one of the most respected and beloved members of the force. At a time when the police of the Los Angeles area were generally considered lawless vigilantes, Adamson stood for all the old-fashioned values. No one would ever believe him capable of the Ripper murders.

Besides, they wouldn't be able to find him; Damien knew that deep in his heart. He wouldn't have taken Lizzie back to L.A., or anywhere they could be traced. They were still out here; he knew it. Just as he knew she would be safe until nightfall.

He had to find her. He was the only one who could. His skepticism was gone, vanished. He couldn't afford to be cynical and rational about it. Hickory had said he had to save Lizzie to atone for the sins of this lifetime and the last. Damien was the only one who could do it, and at last he believed it.

He got in the car and started driving, just driving, aimlessly, too fast. Where would he have taken her? Damien knew this area far better than Adamson ever could—surely he wouldn't be able to keep her hidden.

But the more he thought about it, the more he drove around in circles, as the panic grew and he pictured her lying in a welter of blood, her auburn hair spread out around her lifeless face. He knew what the Ripper did to women. He knew what he'd done to Mary Kelly the first time. He couldn't let it happen to her again.

He stopped thinking. Stopped rationalizing. He only knew he had to save her. He stepped on the gas. The Austin-Healey shot forward with a life of its own, and Damien simply let it go, heading east, deeper into the desert, in search of salvation and the woman he had always loved.

The old train station smelled of dust and mice and old tobacco. The windows were gone, smashed by some itinerant vandal, and the counters had been ripped up, stacked against each other in a random barricade. It was cool inside, in the shade, surprisingly so, considering the brightness of the sun overhead. The winds were still blowing, whipping up the sand and covering everything with a fine layer of silt. It blew in her eyes, gritty and painful, and she could taste it on her tongue.

The closest thing she'd had to solid food since she could remember. Maybe if she ate something she would be able to think things through more clearly. To make sense of what was insane. To find a solution.

She found a spot behind one of the overturned counters. It was dark, a little cul-de-sac, and she pulled out the blanket, settling it on the filthy floor with only a stray shudder, her housekeeping standards long gone.

She curled up there, leaning her head against the wall. Damien wasn't a killer. If someone's hand had written his name in Hickory's blood, then that hand was the Ripper's.

She shouldn't have left. Adamson hadn't been able to keep anyone alive yet—why should he suddenly succeed with her? Especially since he seemed convinced that a man she knew was innocent was the killer.

It made no sense to her. She'd had too little sleep, too little food, too little peace of mind. She wanted to be back with Damien, locked tight in his arms, the night all around them, the demons at bay. She didn't want to be crouched in this deserted building in the bright desert sunlight, waiting for a murderer.

He would find her. She knew it with a sudden clarity that should have terrified her. But she was already past terror. She was here, alone, and the Ripper would come for her. As he had in the past.

She shook her head, trying to banish the fancy that felt so real. She reached into the bag, pulling out a warm can of soda and a cellophane packet of nuts.

Cashews. Long Liz Stride's favorite. Lizzie stared down at them in silent horror. And then she threw them against the wall, and the bag split and cashews spilled all over the floor.

The seconds and minutes and hours blended together in a blur. The desert heat shimmered around her, the hot, dry winds blew through the broken windows, and somewhere in the building she could hear the rustling of mice. She wondered how long it would take them to find the cashews. Not long, she hoped.

She dozed at one point, dreaming about Liz Stride and Mary Kelly and James Killian. None of it made any sense to her, but her dreaming mind tried to sort it out.

She couldn't be two women, and yet she seemed to be. Hickory could have given her the answers. So could Courtland. But they had both fallen beneath the Ripper's knife. As she would.

She was Mary Kelly, not Liz Stride, despite her name, despite her destiny. She knew that now, whether it made sense or not. She was Mary Kelly reborn, though the ghostly spirit of Liz Stride came to visit, to haunt her, as well.

She opened her eyes, suddenly awake. Did the Ripper know he was once more hunting Mary Kelly, the woman on whom he'd committed his foulest butchery? Or was he still looking for Lizzie Stride, to finish what he'd started?

She heard the slamming of a car door, and she realized that the sound of the car was what had awakened her in the first place. The shadows in the deserted train station had lengthened, and dusk was rapidly approaching. When dusk came, somehow the Ripper would claim her. And no white knight would be able to rescue her.

"Lizzie?" It was Damien's voice, raw, panicky, breaking the thick silence of the old building. She could hear him crashing around, and she huddled deeper into her corner, letting the terror surround her. Was Adamson right, after all? How could Damien have found her?

"Lizzie, for God's sake, answer me!" he cried.

He was going to kill her. She accepted that possibility with an unnatural calm. She'd had more than enough time to consider all the possibilities, and if that most unbearable one was the only answer, then she had to accept it. He would find her, huddled in the corner, and she preferred to face him. If she was going to die, she was going to die bravely. Looking into the face of the man she had loved. The man she still loved.

She rose slowly, silently, and for a moment he didn't even see her. She looked at him across the barrier of broken counters and ripped-up benches, stared at him out of wide, accepting eyes, and waited.

"Lizzie," he said, his voice hushed, broken. "He didn't hurt you."

She didn't move. "Who?"

"Adamson. He's the Ripper, Lizzie. I don't know how I could have been too stupid to see it. It has to be him—nothing else makes sense."

"These murders don't make sense," she said, in a low, lifeless voice.

Damien started toward her eagerly, and she took an involuntary step backward, coming up against the wall. She had no place to run, no way to protect herself from him, but her retreat was instinctive.

He saw it and stopped short. "Are you afraid of me, Lizzie?" he asked, in a soft voice. It was warm, seductive, the voice of a lover. The voice of a savage killer.

She looked at him, calmly considering his question. "No," she said finally.

Some of the tension left his wiry shoulders. "You know I wouldn't hurt you," he said, moving closer.

"No," she said. "But I'm not afraid to die."

He stopped, frozen, staring at her through the gathering shadows. She couldn't get away from him; she knew it, and she didn't care. If her destiny was to die at his hands, so be it. She was through fighting it, through trying to guess.

"What did he tell you, Lizzie?" he asked, his voice beguiling.

"That you killed them. You killed them all. Including Hickory."

"Hickory's dead?"

He sounded so shocked. Lizzie just nodded. "He wrote your name in his own blood before he died."

"You were with me when we saw him last, Lizzie. When would I have had time to kill him?"

"I went out to the car first. You came out a minute later. Long enough to cut his throat. Not long enough to make sure he was dead, that he couldn't leave the name of his killer behind."

"Adamson told you this." It wasn't a question, and Lizzie didn't answer it.

"There were witnesses to some of the other killings, people who can identify you. They've found physical evidence."

"What a polite phrase for it," he said, his voice filled with a kind of vicious amusement. "What kind of physical evidence? Hair fibers? Fingerprints? Semen deposits?"

"I thought the women hadn't been raped," she said.

"According to the coroner, if they had sex, someone used a condom. I can't imagine the Ripper practicing safe sex, but anything's possible. But where does that leave you, Lizzie? I had you. You gave yourself to me. There's still proof of that inside your body. Won't that change my evil plans? I can hardly change my modus operandi after more than a hundred years, can I? The Ripper doesn't screw the women he kills—at least not on the same day. Maybe we'll have to wait...."

"Stop it!" she cried, wanting to cover her ears.

He was coming closer, closer, and he had something in his hand. It was a knife, she knew it, and she was ready for it. It would be a relief, the first peace she'd known in her life. She was through running, through fighting. If he wanted to kill her, he could have her.

"Have I got you cornered, Lizzie?" he murmured, his voice a mocking parody of concern. "Nowhere to run to? Nowhere to hide? I always liked Martha and the Vandellas. I wonder if the original Jack used to sing music-hall songs while he did his dirty work? Maybe I need a radio to keep me occupied while I hack you to pieces."

He could touch her. The building was filled with shadows, and he kept his right hand down at his side, hiding the knife from her. She wondered why he bothered. She knew what was coming. She welcomed it.

She leaned against the wall and closed her eyes, waiting. She heard him skirt the pile of wood, felt him approach her, but she refused to look at him. She was ready. But she no longer wanted to look into his eyes when he killed her.

He was close enough that she could hear his tense breathing, feel his body heat, but he didn't touch her. The tension spun out until she couldn't bear it anymore, and she opened her eyes, staring up at him. "Go ahead," she said fiercely. "Do it."

He raised his hand, and there was no knife in it. He reached out for her, and she could see the tension in him. "I want to hurt you," he said, in a low, bitter voice. "I want to slam you against the wall and beat some sense into you." He touched her then, her neck, and his hand was warm and gentle despite his fury. "Damn you, Lizzie." He sank against her, pushing her against the wall, and she could feel his body shake.

Her arms came up around him instinctively. This was no killer. This was no monster. This was the man she loved. "Damien," she said in a broken voice. "I'm so sorry." And she kissed him, her mouth finding his blindly, reveling as he kissed her back with a tightly leashed fury at war with the fierce desire that flared between them.

And then he stiffened in her arms, as if an electric shock had gone through him. "Lizzie," he gasped against her mouth.

Adamson's voice came out of the gathering gloom. "Move away from him, Lizzie."

She clutched at him, and she felt the dampness on his back as he collapsed against her, breathing in short, strangled rasps. "Damien!" she cried.

"Get away from him, Lizzie," Adamson said. "He's a killer. He'd gut you as soon as look at you. You know what he has in his car? Knives. A collection of knives. Oh, and there's a mask there. One of the little girl who looks rather like you. Get away from him, Lizzie, before he kills you."

"Lizzie," Damien breathed in her ear, "run." And then he began to sink, collapsing at her feet, and all her strength couldn't keep him upright.

Her hands were red and slippery with blood. Damien's blood. "What did you do?" she screamed at Adamson. "You're wrong. He wouldn't hurt me."

"No," Adamson said kindly. "But I will." He started toward her, and she saw him raise the bloody knife in his hand, the one he'd already thrust into Damien's back.

But Saucy Jack, Springheeled Jack, Jack the Ripper, misjudged his distance. Lizzie spun around, and the knife slashed down beside her, ripping through her sleeve, tearing into her arm and not her chest, as she ran, leaping over the upended counters, fleet and graceful, faster than the chief inspector had ever been, unhampered by long skirts and corsets. He was after her. She could hear him, but she didn't look back, racing along the pitted and scarred platform, away from the building, away from certain death.

She raced across the old railroad ties, and her foot caught, sending her sprawling. She glanced back as she scrambled to her feet, and he was looming up behind her. His top hat had been lost in the scuffle, and his red-lined cape must have fallen off, but she knew his face, knew it from the last time.

He was screaming at her, words she didn't recognize, and the sounds were horrible, changing from a young boy's cry to a woman's venomous shriek to an old hag's cackle, as he came after her, faster than she would have thought possible.

She didn't know how long she could keep running. Sooner or later he would catch her, sooner or later she would die, as Damien had died, and her only consolation would be that they'd died together. Perhaps they would have one more chance, in some other lifetime.

He was gaining on her. She could see the vague outline of an abandoned truck and she headed for that, hearing him closing in behind her, knowing she would be too late. She'd just reached the rusted hulk when his hand came down on her shoulder, spinning her around, and she looked up into the face of death.

He pulled his hand away from her in horror, as if the touch of her flesh had burned him. "No," he said, in a choked voice. "No. You're the wrong one. Where's Lizzie?"

She thought she could see another shadow on the landscape, moving toward them, but Adamson was too intent to notice. The knife in his hand was huge, glistening wetly with blood, and it would end her life with one slash.

"What do you mean?"

"You're not Lizzie. I know you. You're Mary. Mary Kelly. I don't need you. I already finished with you, centuries ago," he said in a lost voice. "I need Lizzie. Long Liz Stride. They interrupted me, and I never finished. I need to finish. I need to make everything right and proper. I don't even have my mask with me. Damien surprised me, showing up like that. I have to have the mask, you know. Made by Liz Stride's own hands. It's not me, you see," he said confidingly, his tone cozy and horrifying. "He comes and takes over, and I have to wear a mask, just until I find Lizzie Stride. And then I'll be finished, and there'll be no more need for masks. You understand that, don't you, Mary? Tell me where Lizzie is and I promise I won't harm you."

The cold of the desert night bit into her bones. Overhead the stars were bright, and the Santa Ana winds blew through her hair, tossing it in her face.

"Lizzie's gone," she said. "Gone where you can't find her. You'll never hurt her, Adamson."

He stared at her, mute frustration creasing his friendly face. And then he smiled, a ghastly, cheerful smile. "Call me Jack," he said. "And I guess you'll have to do."

The figure came out of the darkness, a hunched-over form releasing a wild cry, leaping onto Adamson like a crazed bat. They went down in a welter of blood and limbs, and the sound that came from their tangled figures was horrifying, a long, low howl that sounded like death.

The top figure staggered away, falling to his knees in the sand, and it was Damien, winded, bleeding, swaying slightly as he stared at Adamson's writhing figure.

"Don't go near him," he said, in a strangled rasp as Lizzie moved, but she had no intention of moving toward the dying man. Instead, she sank to her knees beside Damien and put her arms around him, feeling the wet stickiness of the blood at his back, the painful shudder of his breathing.

The dark figure rolled over and lay there for a moment in the cape of red she'd thought he'd lost. And then Lizzie realized it wasn't a red cape, it was his life's blood flowing out, covering the desert floor. His own knife was embedded in his stomach, and he'd managed to disembowel himself as he'd thrashed around on the blade.

Damien staggered to his feet, keeping an arm around Lizzie, and he moved closer, staring down at the dying man. Adamson's eyes were glazing over, his mouth twisted in a grimace. "It's over," he said, his voice the sigh of death. "This time." And then he lay utterly still, as the last of his blood soaked into the sand beneath him.

"Let's get out of here," Damien whispered, his voice raw with pain.

"We have to get you to a doctor."

"No doctor. I'll be okay. You can take care of it."

"But, Damien, we have to tell someone."

He caught her face, staring down at her, and through the glaze of pain he shook his head. "No one will believe us," he said. "Hell, I don't believe it. No one will solve this Ripper case, any more than they did the original one."

"They'll have questions. They'll find his body...."

"There are coyotes around here. There won't be any trace of him by morning. They'll even drag the bones away."

"Damien..."

"Lizzie," he said. "If they ask us, we'll tell them what we can. But no one's going to ask us. They'll be busy trying to find a trace of Adamson, but the police are a close-knit bunch. If they suspect anything, and sooner or later they're going to have to, they'll cover it up. It's over, Lizzie. No one will ever know who committed these murders, any more than they knew who was the original killer."

"The chief inspector in charge of the investigation," Lizzie said in a quiet voice.

"What makes you say that?"

She looked at him. "I saw him," she said flatly. "I remember."

He didn't say a word. "Let's go away, Lizzie," he said. "Far, far away from here. Let's go someplace where you can make masks and I can write. Where it isn't dark all the time. Let's run away and live this life happily ever after. I love you, Lizzie."

She put her hands on his face, his dear, dark face. Her hands were stained with his blood, but it didn't seem to matter. It simply sealed their fate.

"This time," she said, "we will."

EPILOGUE

The mountains were high and snowy, sharp-peaked, with clean, biting air. The house was low and rambling and very cozy, with wood heat and huge windows to let in the countryside, fresh spring water and power from their own stream. There was no darkness there, and the nights were filled with bright stars lighting their way.

"You're not," Lizzie said, staring at her husband.

"I am."

"You're going to write a book about reincarnation? Are you certain you want to?"

"It'll amuse me," he said, giving her that rare, wonderful smile of his. "Besides, they're paying me a fortune."

"You always told me New Age publishing didn't pay very well," she said.

"It doesn't. My book's debunking the myth of reincarnation. It doesn't exist," he said, his dark eyes alight with amusement.

She just looked at him for a moment. It had been a strange and wonderful year, up in the mountains of New Mexico, away from cities and questions and death. Adamson's body had never been recovered, and it was assumed he'd been the Ripper's final victim. They hadn't closed the case on the Venice Ripper, and probably never would. No one really thought they'd find the answer. But at least the killings had stopped.

She made masks once more, with no fear of death haunting her, and Damien wrote articles for the *Chronicle,* refusing their increasingly lucrative offers to return to the city. Life was clean and simple and very good up here, with good friends and a baby growing in her belly.

"It doesn't exist, huh?" she said, moving closer, leaning against him, and he reached and put his hand across the swelling warmth of their child.

"Nope," he said. "There are no such things as past lives."

"And no such things as second chances?" she murmured.

He tugged her down and kissed her. "I'll convince a large section of the reading public of that," he said.

"You're a swine, James Killian," she said.

"So I am, Mary Kelly." He rubbed her belly. "Just don't tell our daughter that when she's born."

"Don't worry, love," she said, kissing the top of his head. "Courtland will always think her father's perfect." And she leaned down and placed her mouth against his, in a kiss of warmth and peace.

And their long night of darkness was gone forever.

* * * * *

And now from Silhouette Shadows
an exciting preview of

HEART OF THE BEAST
by Carla Cassidy

CHAPTER ONE

He stood at the window, staring out into the blackness of the night. He wished he could meld into the shadows and disappear like the darkness with the coming of the morning sun.

But of course he couldn't, and so he would remain here in this place that had become both his prison and his sanctuary.

"You didn't eat much dinner."

He turned away from the window and stared at the man who had just entered the room. "I wasn't very hungry."

The newcomer nodded and moved over to the portable bar, where he poured two fingers of Scotch into a glass. "Drink?"

The man at the window sat down at a nearby chair and shook his head. "I don't think that's a very good idea, do you?"

"I don't think a small drink of good Scotch would cause any problems."

"I'm not willing to take a chance." The man in the chair leaned back and closed his eyes with a weary sigh.

"She should be here sometime tomorrow."

His eyes flew back open, and he once again stared at the man in front of him. "You really are a monster, aren't you?"

The man tossed back his Scotch in two quick gulps, then, with a humorless smile, looked back at his seated companion. "How amusing that you should call me a monster. Don't you think that's a case of the proverbial pot calling the kettle black?"

The man in the chair clenched his hands into fists, fighting against the anger that began in the pit of his stomach. He knew what anger did to him, and he fought against it with every ounce of inner strength he possessed. But the anger already had a firm grasp, and as it began to unfurl, an insistent prickling sensation attacked his skin. He recognized it immediately: a signal of danger.

"I...must..." He stumbled up from the chair, the prickling sensation now attacking full force.

He pushed past the other occupant of the room, aware only of his immediate need. Very soon he would be completely out of control. His sense of self, the essence of his humanity, would slip away. His head pounded with a nauseating intensity, letting him know the end of rational thought was swiftly approaching.

He stumbled blindly up the stairs and down a long, dark corridor, his breath coming in short, quick gasps.

I must maintain control. I must maintain control. He held on to that thought like a reverent child clutching a crucifix.

It wasn't until he was safely locked into the padded room that he stopped fighting the inevitable. He sank down to the floor and waited for the transformation to begin....

Bonnie Redding shifted her suitcase from one hand to the other, trudging up the deeply rutted road that would lead her to the Redding Institute, her father's home.

Her father... Her heart beat faster at the thought of finally seeing once again the man who'd always held a small part of her heart, but who'd never been more than a minute part of her life.

It had been the death of her mother that had prompted her to come here and find the last remaining family member she had in the world, the man who'd walked out of her life when she was five years old.

She wasn't sure how far she'd walked when she became aware of the silence. It wasn't a normal silence, broken by the rustle of wind-whipped autumn leaves. It wasn't relieved by the scurry of an animal in the underbrush or the call of a bird overhead. It was thick, heavy, oppressive... strange.

Bonnie felt a ripple of unease move up her spine. She'd moved deeper into the woods, where the waning evening light didn't penetrate the shadows of approaching nightfall. The trees were gnarled and twisted, attesting to their age by the width of their massive trunks.

Her footsteps slowed as her gaze darted first left, then right. A prickly sensation itched in the center of her back, the feeling one always got when being watched.

She followed the curve in the road and stopped suddenly, dropping her suitcase and gasping aloud. Constructed mostly of massive gray stones and wood blackened with age, the Redding Institute appeared like a medieval fortress built to withstand the ravages of nature and man. Bonnie shivered. What was her father doing in a place like this?

His letters had mentioned that the institute was large enough to accommodate his laboratory and living quarters for his staff. However, she'd expected a modern building surrounded by cozy cottages. This monstrosity looked like something out of a horror movie, certainly not a place where select scientists worked and lived.

It didn't matter where her father lived. What did matter was her need to connect with him now that her mother was gone.

She walked quickly to the front door, raised her hand to ring the bell, but hesitated, suddenly worried about the reception she'd receive. Her first two letters asking her father if she could come had been answered negatively. He was in the middle of an important project, the timing wasn't right—pages of reasons why she shouldn't come. Then, suddenly, out of nowhere, she'd received a third letter two days ago, encouraging a visit.

Taking a deep breath, she now rang the bell, hearing the chime echoing deep within. Immediately, the heavy door swung open. "May I help you?" a middle-aged woman asked.

"I'm Bonnie Redding. I believe I'm expected."

"Ah, yes. Please come in." A smile moved the woman's lips upward but didn't reach her eyes. "Your father has been anxiously awaiting your arrival. If you'll wait in the library, I'll let him know you're here."

Bonnie nodded, following the woman into a room that, despite the blazing fire in the stone fireplace, offered no sense of welcome.

She stood before the fire, welcoming the warmth the blaze offered. There seemed to be a chill surrounding her.

She turned as the double doors flew open and a gray-haired man in a white lab coat entered.

"Bonnie." He crossed the room in quick strides, stopping before her. "Let me look at you," he said softly, his blue eyes searching her face. "Ah, you're beautiful, the very image of your mother." He reached out and took her hands in his. "I'm so glad you've come."

The words, so long imagined, so desperately yearned for, caused emotion to explode in Bonnie's chest. "I'm so glad I'm here, too," she replied, studying him intently.

"We're just about to sit down to dinner. I'll introduce you to my colleagues."

He took hold of her elbow and led her down the hallway and into a formal dining room. As she took a seat at the table, her father introduced her to the three men—fellow doctors—already seated.

Bonnie's breath caught in her throat as she saw a man standing—no, *filling* the doorway. He was no older than thirty-five. His hair was the color of midnight, curling slightly over his ears and around the nape of his neck. He had bold, dark eyebrows, high cheekbones that threw shadows on the skin below, a straight, aristocratic nose and lips that spoke of an innate sensuality. However, it was his eyes that held her. Pale silvery eyes that gleamed with the cunning of a wild animal, yet held a melancholy that was strangely compelling.

"Ah, Nicholas, you almost missed the soup," Bonnie's father smiled pleasantly.

"I lost track of time." He took the seat at the end of the table. When he looked at Bonnie, gone was the trace of melancholy, and only a cool speculation was visible. "So, you're Walter's daughter."

Bonnie nodded and offered Nicholas a tentative smile, one he didn't return.

Through the entire meal, Nicholas didn't speak a word, but she felt his gaze lingering on her often. She also noticed that the other men watched him covertly, casting surreptitious glances at him. What a strange bunch, she thought. The only one who didn't seem odd was her father.

Bonnie's gaze moved down the table and locked onto Nicholas. He stared at her, and for a moment it was as if all the surroundings faded away and the room only held the two of them.

The silver orbs of his eyes spoke to her, but it was a language she didn't understand. There was danger there, a threat...a warning. There was also another emotion hiding behind his glittering eyes. Like the surface of a pond at sunset, they offered murky depths and hidden mysteries she didn't understand.

A little later, her father led her up a wide stairway to her room.

"It might be a good idea if you stayed away from Nicholas Shepherd. He's brilliant, but there are times I believe his brilliance borders on madness. Well, here we are. I'll leave you to get settled in. There will be plenty of time for us to talk tomorrow." With a slight nod, he closed the door and left the room.

The moment he was gone, Bonnie moved to stand in front of the fireplace. She shouldn't feel disappointed. She really hadn't expected a marathon session of auld lang syne on the first night of her arrival.

She walked over to the mirror that hung above the antique dresser and stared at her reflection, trying to find some vestige of the man who'd just left the room.

Certainly there was no similarity between her own shoulder-length blond hair and her father's steel-gray hair. Her eyes were green, his were blue. Her chin was slightly pointed, his was square. She'd always known that physically she resembled her mother, but she was somehow disappointed that she found not a single physical trait she'd inherited from her father.

After changing into her nightgown, she moved to the window and drew the curtains aside. Opening the doors, she stepped out onto the small balcony.

The moon was halved, casting an eerie illumination over the darkness of the woods. The air was cool, and she wrapped her arms around herself, noting again the utter silence that permeated the area. She'd never heard a silence that sounded so profound, so unnatural.

A branch snapped, the sound exploding out of the quiet like a gunshot in a graveyard. Bonnie's heart banged against her ribs as her gaze sought the cause of the sound.

If the moonlight hadn't been so brilliant, she wouldn't have seen him at all. He looked almost like a shadow blending into the darkness cast from one of the nearby trees.

Nicholas Shepherd. What was he doing out in the woods this time of night? He appeared to be doing nothing, simply standing still, as if he had become a permanent part of the surrounding forest.

Brilliance that bordered on madness.... She remembered her father's words. At that moment he looked up, the moonlight catching his eyes, reflecting up to her. Yes, there was madness there, a haunting, tormented madness that both compelled and repelled.

With a swift intake of breath, she moved back into her room and closed the doors, carefully locking them. She crawled into bed and pulled the covers around her neck. She was cold.... She was suddenly very cold. She closed her eyes, her mind filled with the vision of his eyes shining up at her.

Suddenly a masculine cry split the night. A cry of such torment, such rage that it made her heart seem to stop cold in her chest....

Relive the romance...
Harlequin and Silhouette
are proud to present

A program of collections of three complete novels by the most
requested authors with the most requested themes. Be sure to
look for one volume each month with three complete novels by
top name authors.

In June: **NINE MONTHS** Penny Jordan
                            Stella Cameron
                            Janice Kaiser

**Three women pregnant and alone. But a lot can
happen in nine months!**

In July: **DADDY'S**   Kristin James
            HOME   Naomi Horton
                           Mary Lynn Baxter

**Daddy's Home... and his presence is long
overdue!**

In August: **FORGOTTEN** Barbara Kaye
           PAST   Pamela Browning
                         Nancy Martin

**Do you dare to create a future if you've forgotten
the past?**

Available at your favorite retail outlet.

WHERE WERE YOU WHEN THE LIGHTS WENT OUT?

SILHOUETTE

SUMMER Sizzlers '93

This summer, Silhouette turns up the heat when a midsummer blackout leaves the entire Eastern seaboard in the dark. Who could ask for a more romantic atmosphere? And who can deliver it better than:

**LINDA HOWARD
CAROLE BUCK
SUZANNE CAREY**

Look for it this June at your favorite retail outlet.

Silhouette®

where passion lives.

SS93

Fifty red-blooded, white-hot, true-blue hunks from every
State in the Union!

Beginning in May, look for MEN MADE IN AMERICA!
Written by some of our most popular authors, these
stories feature fifty of the strongest, sexiest men, each
from a different state in the union!

Two titles available every other month at your favorite
retail outlet.

In July, look for:

CALL IT DESTINY by Jayne Ann Krentz (Arizona)
ANOTHER KIND OF LOVE by Mary Lynn Baxter
(Arkansas)

In September, look for:

DECEPTIONS by Annette Broadrick (California)
STORMWALKER by Dallas Schulze (Colorado)

You won't be able to resist MEN MADE IN AMERICA!